Alice in Shadowtime

By the same author

Children's Books
An Edinburgh Reel
The Popinjay
The Burning Hill
The Tree of Liberty
The Snake and the Olive

Non-fiction
Edinburgh and the Eastern Lowlands
Wallace and Bruce
The Importance of Being Earnest (Penguin Passnotes)
Huckleberry Finn (Penguin Passnotes)

Adult Fiction
Death Wore A Diadem

Alice in Shadowtime

IONA McGREGOR

EDINBURGH

© Iona McGregor 1992

Published by Polygon
22 George Square
Edinburgh

Set in Sabon
by Koinonia Limited, Manchester
and printed and bound in Great Britain
by Redwood Press Ltd, Melksham, Wiltshire

The right of Iona McGregor to be identified
as the author of this work has been asserted
by her in accordance with the Copyright,
Designs and Patents Act 1988

British Library Cataloguing In Publication Data
McGregor, Iona
   Alice in Shadowtime
   I. Title
   823.914 [F]

ISBN 0 7486 6134 4

The Publisher acknowledges subsidy
from the Scottish Arts Council towards
the publication of this volume.

Chapter One

Alice Enderby did not intend her father to die when she broke the laws of time. He was murdered on her wedding day and one year before it.

Four hours before his first encounter with Miss Enderby, ex-detective James McLevy alighted at Perth General Railway Station to change to the Highland Line. It was the last Saturday of August 1864, and swelteringly hot. McLevy stood irresolutely in the ticket hall, a bulky man of sixty-two with lively dark eyes and a bald pate fringed by coarse grey hair. He fanned himself with his hat while the dog tugged against a piece of washing line he had looped round her neck. Death was on his mind.

The connecting train for Dunfillan was due to leave in ten minutes. To miss it would be a double breach of duty. He had been barred from the case, and the physician who had ordered him out of town had forbidden even light half-duties.

McLevy walked out of the station.

The streets of Perth pulsated with eye-blinding sunlight. McLevy entered a building and was confronted by a police officer whose face glistened above his loosened collar. A good omen: this was the very man he'd come to question; tall and knobbly, as freckled as a thrush beneath his light brown whiskers, though now sporting a set of stripes. McLevy had been told that Sergeant Kincaid had moved into the city on his promotion.

'Mr McLevy! What brings you to Perth?'

That spring fever had clung like a devil's imp. Its forewarnings of mortality had wrung McLevy's reluctant consent to a month's exile in the country. He explained all this and added, 'A neighbour's cousin offered me lodgings in a village at the head of Glencrannich, so the chance was too good to miss.'

The officer's surprise turned into a knowing grin.

'You've found a new trace on the Sanders murder!'

After six months the enquiry had been closed. A detective officer and the local constable, John Kincaid, had carried the chief constable's decision to Edinburgh.

'Not yet, Johnnie. If I find something I'll persuade the new fiscal to re-open.'

No public prosecutor liked being saddled with his predecessor's cases, but McLevy was an optimist.

Kincaid made a grimace. 'I dinna think Mr Maxwell's the man to stir it.'

'Trust me, Johnnie. I'll nose out something even if the fiscal is more noes than ayes.' Besides a good conceit of himself he had a weakness for lame puns. 'I'm counting on your help – unofficially.'

'There's been neither word nor whisper of our friend, sir.'

'Not even a rumour? You must have heard something in the glen! You've had those only a year.'

Kincaid squinted at his stripes. 'Aye, but I've been in Perth for three. There was a lassie here. We're married now. So when I had the chance...'

As he took the little collie back to the station, McLevy's face fell into glumness. The unsolved case still rankled; it had been almost his last before they put him out to grass. Over the past four years his half-call retirement duties had dwindled almost to nothing.

He had another hour to wait for the next train to Dunfillan. Mysteriously, it was already crammed with two hundred excursionists, and he was lucky to find a perch on six inches of uncushioned planks. As they moved off there was a tepid rush of air through the windows before his carriage began to resemble the Black Hole of Calcutta.

As the train ran beside the glinting silver ribbon of the River Tummel, the passengers swayed in unison with the rhythmic clatter of the wheels, craning for a glimpse of hills through panting clouds of steam.

In May 1860 there had been a tip about an intended robbery in Edinburgh's Royal Mile. His officers seized two of the thieves as they were breaking into the jeweller's cases. Their accomplice jumped out of a window. McLevy had almost overtaken him when the child walked across the street.

The man snatched the jug she was carrying and brought it down on her head. He ran on as McLevy stopped to bend over the small, crumpled body. That was intended, of course, but only the most callous could have hurried by.

Round her the shards of pot were awash with whisky; by the gaslight, slowly overflowing the wet pavement, he could see a darker, thicker stain.

The police officers were waiting for him further down the street having already trussed the man and woman into leather handcuffs. He arranged for the girl to be taken to the Infirmary and set off again in hopeless pursuit.

The girl died a few hours later. She was nine or ten years old. Her first scream had been followed by sounds that could still wake him with a shudder.

When the fugitive was traced to Glencrannich, a remote Highland glen some eight miles west of Dunfillan, he had asked to be sent after him. His superiors said he should stick to Edinburgh business and handed the case over to the Perthshire constabulary. McLevy was to retire that year.

Such meagre results for breaking his journey! He should have caught that early connection. He thought remorsefully how his dog must be suffering inside the guard's van in the added heat of the afternoon. Sweat prickled McLevy's neck as he swallowed to ease his mouth, wishing he had brought a bottle of ale.

Well, it had been worth a try. He elbowed a few extra inches and opened his guidebook.

GLENCRANNICH: *a romantic and solitary expanse, its declivitous precipices in some parts never admitting a ray of sunshine in the winter months. Most of the shooting rights of the glen are attached to Kilcorrie House, one of the seats of the Earl of Dunfillan.*

'That's a fib for a start,' said an English voice beside him. He had ignored his neighbours, too aware of their intimate proximity.

The woman was in early middle age, dressed in a straw bonnet and plaid-patterned dress. There was a basket clutched on her lap and she had been reading across his shoulder.

'Kilcorrie House belongs to Mr Enderby now. They ought to say so.'

McLevy learned that his stay in Glencrannich was to be enlivened by Alice Enderby's wedding. He did not welcome the news. Now there were such poor prospects for the Sanders case he was resigned to mental hibernation for the sake of his health.

The bride had already joined her father in the Highlands. Her mother was travelling with all the bridal paraphernalia in a reserved family saloon which Mrs Abigail Vesey had been unable to join. After seeing to the baggage she'd been lucky to struggle on at all. A miracle she'd survived the past month, her being up and down like a Bow Street Runner. Not to mention the accident with her and Miss Alice.

'Three o'clock, just outside York. The flying Scotch

Express. Flying too fast if you ask me. Went clean off the rails.'

'Neither of you was injured, I hope?'

'Miss Alice made us catch the night train. But didn't I wish we stayed at Palace Gate till the end of August!'

'Palace Gate?'

'Kensington,' said Mrs Vesey witheringly. 'You're Irish, ain't you? You can't be long over from Dublin.'

'Madam, for the past thirty-three years I have served in the Edinburgh city police.'

'Peeler? I made sure you was a farmer.'

McLevy pushed himself deeper into the corner.

As the train shrieked its arrival at Ballinluig the unified mass of humanity began to pull apart. Most of the passengers stumbled out. The sound of a brass band rendering 'The Killiecrankie March' was counterpointed by baa-ing from the rear, where a truck of sheep was being hitched on for the Pitlochry sales.

McLevy lay back, letting his body expand into its normal shape. He shut his eyes against the glare, and Mrs Vesey removed herself to a seat opposite. He fended off her offer of a pork pie but accepted some ginger beer, napping through a catalogue of the Enderby trousseau.

It was Mrs Vesey's shaking that woke him. The guard was unlocking the door.

'I'll wave goodbye, dear.'

The board outside read DUNFILLAN.

McLevy seized his carpet-bag and followed her to the platform stepping into the shade of the slatted roof while he felt for his ticket. The engine was being disconnected for its run to the water tower, and a dozen other passengers stood stretching their arms and taking deep breaths of the pure air for which the district was famous.

The squeak of porters' trolleys was drowned in barking as a flurry of dogs leapt out of the guard's van with their zinc labels rakishly awry and rushed to their owners.

McLevy went to the van and whistled. Sidling out, Jeanie Brash dropped to the platform and crawled towards him. She sprang into his arms, whimpering with relief. He lowered the little black and tan collie to the ground, and she feathered herself round his ankles. He was glad she kept so close; he didn't want to put the rope on her again, and her collar and lead had been accidentally left behind in Edinburgh. He had named her Jeanie Brash after his most audacious thief.

A horse-drawn omnibus waited outside the station, beyond which McLevy saw whitewashed houses framed by the outline of the ruined cathedral. As he walked to the ticket gate his eyes were caught by a pair who had the look of father and daughter. The man was fifty-fiveish, ruddy-faced and balding, dressed in a kilt and shooting jacket. He was waving his glengarry bonnet.

Mrs Vesey helped a middle-aged woman out of the train. Behind her emerged a young man in country clothes. The man and his daughter advanced towards them, the young woman clinging to her father's arm and advancing in a series of skips. The two of them stopped in front of McLevy.

He could see none of the milk-and-roses fragility suggested by Mrs Vesey's chatter. Alice Enderby was almost as tall as her fiancé, with an alert, strong face, well shaped and bony. McLevy was struck by the contrast between the face and the childlike gestures.

The girl tugged at her father's arm.

'I said Mama would travel in blue!'

The childish tone did not fit the maturity of her voice. McLevy's torpor gave way to curiosity. Even her bridegroom wasn't what he expected. According to Mrs Vesey Captain Hatterton had recently bought himself out of a Hussar regiment. This man showed not a trace of a cavalry moustache. Instead, his features had that sarcastic, clever mobility he associated with those who waged battle in wig and gown. The young man's smile was genuine. Mrs Vesey's hints that the captain was after the family money were surely mistaken.

Miss Enderby checked herself from running towards him, and when the two couples met exclaimed, 'Jack! I did not think you would travel with Mama.'

'Dear Alice, of course I must attend your wedding.'

He placed a measured kiss on her cheek.

Did they share an unusual sense of humour? Miss Enderby kissed her mother, and, looking around at the other passengers, put a question which McLevy did not catch. The answer – whatever it was – took the light out of her face.

McLevy passed out of the railway station behind Mrs Vesey.

'A handsome couple,' he murmured, not loud enough for her employers to hear. 'They should look well in the bridal victoria as well.'

The lady's maid giggled.

'You silly! That isn't Miss Alice's sweetheart. That's Mr Douglas.'

Chapter Two

An hour after her arrival Rose Enderby was steeping herself in a hip bath in her bedroom at Kilcorrie. The swagged velvet curtains framed a vista of parkland and mountain peaks, but Mrs Enderby had turned her back on the view. With her right foot she was bobbing the sponge up and down and trying to ignore the shreds of peat that floated in the topaz-coloured water.

Mrs Enderby faced the hardest task of her life. She had less than a week in which to crush her husband's passion for his Highland estate. The water churned as she rubbed the sponge up and down her chubby legs. She and Harry had penetrated only the fringes of London society; her grandchildren must inhabit it by right. She had endured four autumns in North Britain to bring about this match. After the wedding she intended never again to cross the Scotch border.

A murmur of voices, all of them male, rose from the terrace. These were Harry's sporting friends; Alice had written that after their exploits on the moor most of them yawned their way through dinner and slumped into bed.

Mrs Enderby stretched over the rim for a towel which she draped round herself before rapping three times on the side of the bath. Her husband entered. He sat on the edge of the bed to watch her dry herself. His wife noted how remote his glance was, although he had not seen her for several weeks.

Rose Enderby never used the services of a lady's maid. After putting on her chemise she pointed behind her back. Henry stood up to lace the whalebone corset.

His touch was efficient and impersonal. 'Too tight?'

'No, dear.' Mrs Enderby had sighed. Her resentment was curbed by memories of how the lacing used to be interrupted. At Kilcorrie her husband's energy was devoted solely to his sport.

'What did you want to see me about?

'Wait till I'm dressed, dear!'

'I wish you'd come down three weeks ago, Rosie. Alice has been run off her feet. I've hardly seen her except at dinner.'

'I'm sure Alice has managed perfectly well.' Mrs Enderby stepped into her dinner gown, and her tone became fretful. 'Why can't the Scotch splice people in church the same as everyone else?'

'It's all perfectly legal. Don't start fussing again.'

'When *is* Miles coming back from York?'

'Monday. His aunt's recovering.'

'I don't believe she's ill at all. She did it to spite us.'

'Isn't twenty thou a year worth a bit of dancing?'

'Provided she doesn't change her mind.'

Mr Enderby helped his wife with the hooks of her gown.

'What if she does? There's plenty for both of them. You used to be so good at book-keeping when we started on our own, Rosie. Why can't you understand?'

'That was different,' said his wife flatly. Twisting up the light brown strands of her hair she began to decorate it with flowers from the bouquet on her dressing-table. After a few moments she removed the hairpins from her teeth; she had decided to speak her mind.

'I think you should discuss the lease of the estate with Miles before he and Alice are married.'

'But I'm giving him Bucksteads outright.' This was his property in Sussex.

'I mean Kilcorrie.'

'Good God, Rosie!'

Mrs Enderby quailed at his vehemence. She pretended he was balking at her impetuosity. 'Perhaps you'd prefer to leave the contract till they return from their wedding tour. It could still be announced at the wedding breakfast.'

Mr Enderby began to fidget round the room with a look of hangdog unhappiness. His wife was reassured. She was usually able to wear him down.

'Harry, we'd all be more comfortable if you'd go back to walking up partridges nearer London. You could still come down to Scotland in September.'

He overlooked the pronoun. 'We couldn't count on Miles asking us.' His voice became plaintive. 'I rebuilt Kilcorrie for you. It's the family home.'

'It still would be if you gave it to Miles.' Suddenly her patience was exhausted. 'You can't hold on to the estate for ever!'

He faced her with a half-smile, as if she had made some false move. 'Why didn't you bring this up before? It's rather late now, Rosie.'

She could feel her neck and cheeks flooding with heat. 'How could I bring it up before? I've always agreed for Alice's sake.' Eligible bachelors went north in August; it had been necessary to follow them. 'Let's talk about it tomorrow,' she called out as her husband left the room.

Rose Enderby went to the window, and confronted the view. She loathed her Highland home. The vastness outside overwhelmed her. She had no country interests and never took part in the walking or sketching parties made up by her women guests. After giving the servants their orders she could only fold her hands and wait for dinner. Sometimes she felt she would die of boredom. Once she had caught herself wishing that her husband might meet with some accident on the moor.

It had been a terrible mistake to let Harry buy Kilcorrie. In that dreadful winter of 1860 she had been too distraught to foresee the difficulties it would cause. How unjust life was! She had been a dutiful wife for twenty years, submitting to all Harry's whims. But the annual trek to Scotland had turned out to be unnecessary: Miles and Alice had met in London.

Chapter Three

Jimmy Dewar walked into the outskirts of the village swinging his tool-bag jauntily. He had wriggled out of a tight corner, although it was only by luck he'd discovered what the McIvers were up to.

For the past six days he'd been working on the outcrop at the top of Kilcorrie woods. Saturday morning he'd risen an hour earlier than usual. This wee chap had come stotting through the trees, the laird himself, it turned out. Seemingly he always walked this road before his breakfast.

'Who are you?'

'Jimmy Dewar, sir, the jobbing mason frae Dunfillan.' Standing up with his cap off. It paid to be souple with the gentry.

The laird prodded the millstone with his stick. 'Who the devil told you to cut this?' He spat out the words like he was cutting them with cheese-wire. 'Didn't Brodie explain you're to mend the walls at Bealach nan Bo?'

'Walls, sir?'

'Dykes, I suppose you'd call them. For the deer drive on Thursday. The – ah – tinchel at my daughter's wedding.'

Hector McIver hadn't mentioned the dykes.

'You may continue here for the rest of the day. See that you get up the hill on Monday.'

'Right, sir.' Behind Jimmy's wooden tone, his mind was racing. He'd reported for work at the big house on Monday morning, but the Kilcorrie gamekeeper was in a hurry to ride up to the deer lodge. He said his assistant would tell Jimmy what had to be done.

The chap hadn't turned up, so at nine Jimmy walked back to the inn where he was to lodge. He was getting on fine with the landlady's daughter when in came this Hector McIver, explaining that his brother was up on the high tops looking out beasts for the tinchel; he'd asked Hector to pass on Brodie's orders about the new millstone and take him to the outcrop. Hector promised Jimmy an extra half-crown if the stone was finished before the wedding.

Jimmy hadn't seen Hector again until yesterday forenoon, Friday. He suddenly appeared at the outcrop and invited him for supper on Saturday evening. The McIvers' cottage lay halfway between the big house and the village, just off the road that went through the Pass of Crannich. Hector said he'd see Jimmy caught the post-gig to Dunfillan; it would save him the eight-mile walk.

The arrangement suited Jimmy fine. It was a damned long trek to the big house for his supper every night and then back to the Dunfillan Arms at Kilcorrie to sleep. Isa was expecting him home for Sunday.

At first he'd taken both the invitation and the extra pay as kindness, in spite of Hector's sour looks. He should have kent better.

He'd wanted to discover what the McIvers were up to, so he got his supper off them. It soon came clear. The meal was to stop him telling how he'd cut the millstone instead of mending the laird's dykes. Poor daft bodies. He could have blabbed any night he'd taken his supper at Kilcorrie, and wasn't it bound to come out sometime?

A thrawn, twisted deil of a man, yon Hector McIver! And him a kirk elder, if you could credit it. He'd not let him play a trick like that again.

Mary Gregory, the landlady's daughter, had hinted that Hector had an ill will at the laird. He must be trying to hold up the repair work, just to spoil the tinchel. Daft!

As he entered the Dunfillan Arms to collect his dirty linen Jimmy's thoughts turned to something else that was bothering him. Mrs Gregory had said that when he returned on Monday he would have to share his room with an Edinburgh policeman.

Jimmy had good reasons for keeping clear of the law.

Chapter Four

McLevy had expected a thatched bothy. The arrangement was ten shillings a week, all found. That was the most he could spare from his pension. The omnibus drew up in the main street of the village in front of a slated two-storey building whose painted sign advertised *The Dunfillan Arms, proprietrix Mrs Isobel Gregory.*

The landlady showed him into a small room on the first floor, saying it was normally used to store linen.

'I hope you'll no object to sharing when the mason's back frae Dunfillan.'

After unpacking his carpet-bag McLevy went to eat in the kitchen, while Jeanie buried her muzzle in a bowl of scraps by the fire.

He was amused by the likeness between the landlady and her daughter, both blonde in complexion and consciously vain of their fine figures. Mrs Gregory retained the accent of her native Falkirk. Mary, born and bred in the glen, laughed and chattered in both English and Gaelic.

A great number of young men found urgent reasons to look into the kitchen. Mary flirted with them all, but her heart was not in it until the arrival of a good-looking lad in his early twenties, curly-headed and with the high colour of someone who spent most of his time in the open air.

'Donald! You're no allowed Saturday nights!' cried Mrs

Gregory. 'We've our hands full with the summer visitors.'

Donald laughed and kissed Mary.

'Can he no come back when we've finished?' she pleaded.

Mrs Gregory relented. 'So long's it's no before eleven... Only if you're out of my sight in two seconds, Donald McIver!'

The young man kissed Mary again, and whispered something which produced a soft giggle as he departed.

The landlady explained, 'They're to be married in March, when Donald gets Rob Brodie's place. He's the head keeper up at Kilcorrie.'

She was less stern with one older visitor who went straight to the fire and bent his nut-brown face over the soup pot.

'Excellent, Isobel! But still not the true mulligatawny. There is your special broiled salmon to follow?'

'You ken fine there is. Has Ritchie seen to your horse, Balinmore?'

The man's brass-buttoned coat had a naval air; he was wearing a wig. Turning to go, he clapped on one of those wide-brimmed hats known as 'wideawakes', and paused in the doorway to address Mary in what McLevy realised was fluent Gaelic.

'What did he say to you ?' asked her mother.

The girl laughed. 'That nonsense he told me before, but it was for you he meant it. Mr McLevy, my mother keeps our best bedroom for Balinmore every Saturday night.'

Mrs Gregory's stirring of the soup became more vigorous.

'It's just his way of speaking. He was a surgeon in the navy.'

McLevy hid a smile. 'Sailors are hearty fellows.'

'Balinmore is his place at the head of the glen,' went on Mrs Gregory. 'Folk also cry him "Dr Sandy" and "Mr McLaren"'.

'Yet it is the one man only,' added her daughter; she looked McLevy straight in the eye.

He decided that Mary Gregory was not so innocent after all.

After supper he took Jeanie Brash for a stroll along the glen, again restraining her with the length of rope in case she ran away. It was not needed. She crept behind him, her nose nervously snuffing the air. The calmness of the evening at last reassured her and she began to trot at McLevy's heel.

The sky brimmed with that golden blue light particular to the central Highlands, but the native fauna were biting sharply. McLevy lit his pipe as he surveyed these new surroundings.

The hotel was at the Dunfillan end of the village, and next to it was the parish church which gave the place its name, Kirkton of Kilcorrie. The church was overhung by one huge beech tree, its ancient branches shading the whole graveyard.

The village consisted of a general shop, a blacksmith's forge, and a few houses, most of them thatched with broom. The fields across the road were enclosed by a continuous stone wall running down to the river. Two had been cut for hay, but the rest were all laid out for potatoes and turnips.

McLevy stood at the end of the gravelled street, while the little collie lifted her muzzle hopefully. He pulled at her ears.

'You're brave enough now, lass!'

The road up the glen swept round the grounds of a roofless castle surrounded by barns and other outbuildings. The gates had been wrenched off their stone pillars and beyond them the overgrown drive was marked out by an avenue of trees cut down to stumps.

McLevy had a whim to view the declivitous precipices

promised by his guidebook, and walked on until he saw the road lose itself in thick woods overhanging the river. Two mountains loomed above it to form the Pass of Crannich. He pressed on, ignoring the weariness that dragged at his legs.

The ascent into the woods was harder than he had expected, and the road was crooked as well as steep. He kept well away from its left-hand side; there the tree crests disappeared with alarming suddenness. Far below, he could hear the invisible river.

He felt easier when the road levelled out, with the Crannich running beside it, and he decided to walk a half-mile more. The trees still clustered thickly on the other side of the river, but to his right there was now a broad stretch of parkland backed by hills rising out of plantations of larch and beech. Set against them was a white house with castellated parapets; an avenue of beeches curved from the road towards it, and he passed a set of ornamental iron gates a hundred yards further on.

He was puzzled; according to the guidebook Kilcorrie should have been a small seventeenth-century tower-house. He sat down on a boulder, rather abruptly. His legs were shaking. He brought out his pipe again, angry at his own weakness. After a ten-minute rest he'd walk back and spend the rest of the evening in Mrs Gregory's taproom.

There was a rattle of approaching wheels; a one-horse vehicle was being driven towards him. McLevy waved his hat, and the driver stopped. It was a postal gig.

'Like a hurl to the village, sir?'

Thankfully, McLevy pulled himself up to the box, and Jeanie jumped up beside him.

The summer visitors kept to themselves in their parlour; the taproom was used by local crofters and shepherds.

McLevy sat by the empty fireplace, minding his own business. He would need the greatest caution in easing himself into this small community. They would play dumb if they guessed what he was after.

The men talked about the harvest. Two of them complained that Mr Enderby had taken them off their own crofts to prepare the bonfires for the wedding. This topic was hushed up by the third.

A dark-bearded man, neither young nor old, entered and sat opposite McLevy. He nodded at the others without speaking. Mary drew him some ale and brought it over. She held out her hands.

'Do they smell of fish?'

The man smiled grudgingly.

Mary brushed her hands up and down the sides of his face.

'Donald would not be so slow to answer.'

The man pushed her hands away and lifted the tankard to his mouth, drinking slowly.

'I am not Donald.'

'A bonny lassie,' said McLevy, when Mary returned to the kitchen.

The bait was rejected. 'She clacks too much.'

As a clock chimed in another part of the hotel, the man took out his watch. He emptied his tankard and stood up.

There was the sound of raised voices in the outside passage; Mary and her mother were arguing with someone.

'Never mind the reason,' came from Mrs Gregory. 'I'm fair vexed at you!'

Donald McIver broke into the room and seized the man's lapels. 'I have words to say to you, Hector, and not good ones!'

'What are you at, you fool? Could you not wait till I came home?'

The crofters turned to stare and grin; the black-bearded man pushed Donald out of the room. Someone rose and followed the quarrelling pair into the corridor. There were sounds of a scuffle and abusive words, but they died away outside the building.

A few moments later the crofter returned with a broad smile on his face. 'Young Donald will have an eye as purple as a bramble berry.'

'What was it all about, Ewan?'

The three heads drew together. There was laughter as Ewan explained, changing between English and Gaelic, but too low for McLevy to make out the words. One of them said reprovingly, 'He should ken better at his age. Him with all thae bairns to feed.'

Mrs Gregory entered with a tight look on her face. She stood behind the bar until the conversation returned to the harvest.

McLevy was not displeased to be awakened twice that night. The spring fever had caused a slight deafness, and it was a relief to find that his ears were as sharp as ever.

On the first occasion, in the darkness and silence of the Highland night, he heard an owl hunting over the graveyard.

Later he was disturbed by the creaking of boards in the corridor. He hurled himself out of bed and opened the door before remembering that he was not on duty.

A light was glimmering from Mrs Gregory's bedroom, where the door stood ajar. It was cut off as Dr Sandy slipped inside.

Chapter Five

Alice Enderby gazed at Alice Enderby; their arms rose to touch their hats, but, to Alice, not quite simultaneously.

Mrs Vesey said, 'Don't forget your gloves, Miss Alice.'

Alice began to smooth the white kid over her fingers. Mrs Vesey smiled at her in the mirror.

'Only one day more. If they ran Scotch trains like in a Christian country you'd have your sweetheart with you this very afternoon. I'll tell the mistress you're ready.'

After Mrs Vesey left the room Alice went on looking at her reflection. The other Alice made a sudden gesture; Alice's gloved hand lifted in response

Why now, when she was so full of joy and longed for her wedding day? Dr Henschel had dismissed it as a nervous weakness. He had sat beside her in front of a mirror.

'There! Do you see?' she demanded.

The doctor exchanged glances with her mother.

'My dear Miss Enderby, there is no anticipation, not even by the fraction of a second. Look –' He twirled his side-whiskers. 'Thus I produce the same effect. You see only an obedient reflection.' But Alice knew he was only humouring her.

She heard him whisper on the way out, 'Temporary moral insanity.' Mama told everyone it was green sickness.

Alice-the-disobedient-reflection had tormented her for

about six months before disappearing from her mirror. She hadn't returned for more than three years, until this present visit to Kilcorrie. Alice had been careful not to be alone with Papa, afraid she might be tempted to confide in him. It would be wrong to make him anxious. Mama mustn't be told either in case she whispered it to Miles. He might stop loving her.

The reflection had begun to misbehave on November 1st, 1860, which was Papa's birthday. Alice could remember vividly the occasions when it had mocked her, but not their sequence or date. To both Papa and Mama she pretended she remembered nothing about her illness. This was only partly a fib; she had forgotten almost everything between October 1860 and the end of the following March. Between those dates her diary was full of illegible scribbles. Sometimes a shadow of recollection crept to the back of her mind; then her heart would begin to pound, and panic drove it away.

Mama had told her that the illness began on their first holiday in Scotland.

Alice often thought that there were half a dozen Alice Enderbys inside her, many of them happily vanished. It had been wrong to poke fun at Mama for her slips in grammar. If Papa hadn't been so clever they might still have been living in one of those houses off Shoreditch High Street she had entered with Jack.

She had said so once to Abby, who replied very tartly, 'That's bosh, Miss Alice. Your Mama and Papa was always very snug and respectable. I do wonder, really, Mr Douglas taking you into such places!'

'My dear, Abby tells me you are ready.'

Mrs Enderby had entered the room, and now sat down beside Alice at the dressing-table.

'Is it time to go to church, Mama?'

'No, Papa has only this minute sent for the carriage. Dearest, I have a question to ask you. I want you to be very, very truthful with me.'

'Am I not always so, Mama?' Alice knew that she was giving the special look that brought on Mama's warmest smile.

'Of course you are, my darling. Do you enjoy being at Kilcorrie?'

This was the solemn, stilted tone which Mama put on for dinner parties and receptions. It was used among themselves only in the gravest circumstances.

'Mama, you know how dearly I love our Highland home. The mountains are wild and beautiful, and the countryfolk seem so contented.'

'Please don't be satirical, my dear one.'

Alice was amazed. She had not intended that at all.

Mama went on, 'I shall share a secret with you. Papa intends to lease Kilcorrie to Miles.'

Alice clapped in delight. 'When did he tell you?'

'Papa never speaks until his mind is quite made up. I am sure he is considering such a plan.'

'Then I must pretend to be surprised.'

'Think about this carefully, Alice. You would have to live here most of the year until Miles inherits from his aunt. I shall discourage Papa, unless I am sure you would be happy.'

'Mama, I should like it ever so!'

'That's settled, then, my darling.'

Alice noticed the relief in her mother's voice; she was not sure whether this was because she now sounded sincere, or because she had agreed with her.

'Try to raise the subject with Papa before the wedding. You can remove his doubts better than I.'

'Doubts?'

Mama hesitated. 'I mean he would be more contented if he heard it from your own lips.'

Mrs Enderby put her arm round her daughter's waist, and, so entwined, they went downstairs to the waiting carriage.

'Good-day to you, McLevy. My sister wishes to meet you.'

In his Sabbath black the man was indistinguishable from others now filing into Kilcorrie church. When he lifted his stovepipe hat McLevy recognised Dr Sandy. He had already decided to approach the parish minister; attending the Sunday services would be an excellent way to begin their acquaintance. McLevy had walked to the church with Mrs Gregory, who now exclaimed, 'How are *you* away from your own kirk, Balinmore?'

It must be usual for Dr Sandy to make a tactful disappearance on Sunday mornings.

'A compliment to the bride, Isobel. Her last appearance among us as Miss Enderby. Miss McLaren is joining me.'

The same reason seemed to have attracted a huge congregation. Mrs Gregory expressed surprise: she whispered that apart from summer visitors Mr Bisset usually drew in only a few worshippers.

The Kilcorrie party was the last to enter.

The precentor gripped his tuning fork as the minister mounted the pulpit. He was a youngish, ugly-featured man, with a mellifluous voice.

Fifteen minutes into the sermon, a low but savage growling rose from the back of the church, and some children began to scream. McLevy turned round; Jeanie Brash was creeping up the aisle, nose probing the air, her lips snarled back to the gums. He carried her outside. 'Sorrow on you, you noisy besom!'

Jeanie continued to growl under the tight pressure of his arms until they were inside the Dunfillan Arms. He shut her in his bedroom and returned to the church, deeply embarrassed.

When the congregation dispersed Dr Sandy approached him again. 'Miss McLaren and I have taken a private room between services. I hope you'll eat with us, McLevy.'

While waiting for the meal, they walked towards the Pass of Crannich, followed by an aged pointer bitch which Miss McLaren had brought in the dogcart.

'Just a companion now. Too old for sport. An unmarried man should always keep a dog,' pronounced Dr Sandy. 'Where's yours?'

McLevy explained that Jeanie had been put under lock and key to prevent her escaping again. He asked, 'Who was that dour-looking fellow standing at the collection plate?' He had recognised the man who had quarrelled with Donald McIver.

'That's Bisset's senior elder, Hector McIver. Donald's brother.'

'A kirk elder!' McLevy described the scene he had witnessed on Saturday night. 'He seems to have an air of perpetual grievance.'

'Hector's had ill luck. The last minister persuaded his father to let him try for a college bursary, and coached Hector himself, but that lasted only six months. Old McIver was killed by a falling tree, the same year I left the navy. Hector had to return to the glen to work the croft. Then their mother died. There's a whole hen-coop of youngsters to bring up. Janet, the eldest sister, keeps house for the family.'

'Very ill luck,' agreed McLevy.

'Hector's a rum chap. Can't reef his sails to the wind. Everything marks him like my old pate.'

Dr Sandy ducked sideways, pulling off hat and wig together, and displayed a reddish scalp corrugated into tightly seamed ridges. Its whole surface was pitted with minute black dots.

'Great heavens, Mr McLaren! How did that happen?'

'Navarino in 1827, when I was a middy. Never had a hair on my head since. See the grains of gunpowder? Decided to go back as a surgeon.' Dr Sandy replaced his wig and hat.

'Does Mr Enderby own the whole glen?'

'Only up to Inverconan. The McLarens have always held Balinmore.' There was more than a touch of Highland pride in this remark. 'Time for our meat, McLevy. Let's turn back.'

Flora McLaren was ten years older than her brother, tall and bespectacled. At first, McLevy perceived her in a spirit of caricature. A reader of *Punch*, he was not immune to its prejudice against outspoken spinsters.

The three of them were waited on by Mrs Gregory. McLevy found this very odd. Did Miss McLaren know about her brother's Saturday nights?

'Do you shoot or fish yourself, Mr McLevy?' asked Flora.

He hastily thrust aside his wonderings. 'No, ma'am. My prey runs on two legs and flies without wings.'

Flora said she had purchased his memoirs for the Balinmore library, and McLevy changed his opinion. The McLarens could be two valuable allies. He mentioned the Sanders case.

'Oh, I remember it well,' said Flora. 'That poor child. The police would not reveal why they believed the murderer had come to Glencrannich.'

'His accomplices peached, Miss McLaren. He was a recent acquaintance, and not a native of Edinburgh. He told them he was on his way to his folk in Glencrannich.'

Dr Sandy said, 'I cannot think of any family who received a relation from Edinburgh four years ago.'

'Perhaps the person is a distant cousin and is still in hiding.'

'This isn't the age of the Jacobites, Flora! The man may have emigrated by now.'

'Who are your incomers for the past four years?' asked McLevy.

'Offhand I should say the Enderbys, their gamekeeper,

the parish minister, one of my own tenants, and Mrs Gregory's kitchen lass.'

One must indulge a man whose scalp has been fried off his head at the age of seventeen. McLevy let several waggish remarks go by before explaining himself.

'My dog was with me when I was called to the robbery. She seized the man's cuff. He shook her off so violently that he heuked out one of her teeth, poor brute. Jeanie has a photographic nose.'

'That terrible growling this morning! The criminal was at Mr Bisset's service!' Flora's eyes sparkled. 'I wonder whether it is man or woman.'

He was disconcerted at her quickness; he replied sombrely, 'No female could deliver such a blow.'

Flora returned a chilling look. 'Anyone will find the will and strength to kill, if desperate enough.'

Chapter Six

As McLevy's train was departing from Edinburgh his sister Mary had called out that she would forward Jeanie's collar and lead to Dunfillan. On Monday morning Mrs Gregory's stableman had to drive into the town for supplies, and offered a place in the inn dogcart. McLevy decided to spend the day looking round Dunfillan and return by omnibus. Jeanie Brash was left behind.

They found themselves following the Kilcorrie victoria, which clattered past the inn just as Mrs Gregory was giving Ritchie his final instructions.

As McLevy entered the stationmaster's office he caught sight of Jack Douglas walking up and down the booking hall with Mrs Vesey. Alice was on her way to the platform with her mother. The lead and collar had arrived with a piece of paper wrapped round them. McLevy sat down to read Mary's letter. He heard Mrs Vesey say, 'Is that the captain's train?'

He looked up and saw her trail a finger down one of the timetables pasted to the wall.

Jack scowled. McLevy made himself drop his eyes to the letter again. He felt intense curiosity about the Enderby household.

Before he had read beyond 'Dear James –' Mrs Vesey's voice again caught his ear.

'There's that Edinburgh peeler, him I met on the train.

Have I time to speak to him?'

She ran towards him, and McLevy rose to his feet. While he was explaining what had brought him to Dunfillan, Alice Enderby returned to the booking hall and went to speak to Jack Douglas.

The young man then walked over and lifted his hat.

'Mr McLevy, my name is Douglas. Miss Enderby wishes me to enquire whether you would care to join us in our day's excursion. That is, if you have no other engagements.'

The invitation was as improbable as the coincidences in a sensation novel. Mrs Vesey's mouth opened in surprise. When the four of them had seen Mrs Enderby on to the train and were seated in the victoria McLevy heard that the original plan had been for Abby Vesey to travel into Perth with Mrs Enderby to make final arrangements with the caterers. Jack and Alice had intended only to accompany them to the station. The plan had been changed by Alice, and Mrs Enderby had agreed, on condition that Abby remain behind.

'It would be a shame to return to Kilcorrie on such a beautiful day. I have never seen the Pass of Killiecrankie or the Falls of Tummel. Mama said that Abby is to be our chaperon.'

The two others seemed used to indulging her, although Jack Douglas raised a mild objection.

'Should we drive so far, Alice? That doesn't sound very restful for the horses.'

'They can be stabled while we have luncheon.'

'I see. The last ride together.' He gave a quick smile, as if conscious of indiscretion.

'But not *for ever ride*,' capped Alice, evidently well up in the works of Mr Robert Browning. 'We must meet Mama's train when she returns from Perth.' Her face glowed. 'I expect Miles will be on it. He is travelling from Edinburgh this morning. He had to spend two days there on family business.'

As the coachman drove towards Pitlochry Mrs Vesey asked what was famous about 'that Killie place'.

McLevy described the battle and the death of Bonny Dundee while observing the interplay between Jack and Alice. Of course the young man was in love with her. He was not sure whether Miss Enderby was aware of this; their intimacy seemed the product of long acquaintance.

The woods were already steeped in autumn tints; to their left the river gave out a throaty roaring. As they drove through the splashes of sunshine, Alice's face under her parasol took on an ambiguous expression; her mouth seemed to smile when her eyes were grave, and her eyes sparkled when the rest of her face was still. She appeared happy, but there was some strain beneath her smiles. McLevy was reminded of the silky pluminess of a bird layered so thinly above its fragile case of bone.

His account of the Battle of Killiecrankie lasted until they were driving along the main street of Pitlochry.

'Let's ask the people at the hotel for a luncheon basket,' said Alice. 'We shall take a picnic at the falls.'

Abby Vesey was sent into the hotel to give the order, while the others waited in the open carriage.

Alice said, 'Abby tells me you are a famous detective, Mr McLevy.'

So Mrs Vesey had been enquiring about him. 'I have been moderately lucky in my career.' Immodestly modest, he dismissed his two thousand convictions.

Mrs Vesey reappeared with a young lad in page's buttons who was carrying a wicker hamper. After this had been strapped to the floor of the carriage they set off again.

'They said it's a mile and a bit to Garry Bridge, Miss Alice, and then we turn left for the falls. We have to walk through the woods.'

'Very well, we shall have luncheon at Garry Bridge. Tell us about one of your cases, Mr McLevy. A blood and thunder murder, if you please!'

'Little blood, and most of the thunder proceeded from the bench. I dealt with stolen goods, Miss Enderby.'

She looked so disappointed that he searched for a tale to please her. There had been that gruesome find of a child's leg in a High Street soil pipe; and Miss Balleny of Buccleuch Street, battered out of her wits by an intruder. Neither was suitable entertainment for ladies.

He chose an incident softened by a tinge of the supernatural.

'In 1835 I had to arrest a cobbler named William Wright who stabbed his best friend with a knife during an argument.'

'Fancy that!' cried Mrs Vesey. The two women settled back in comfortable anticipation.

'The extraordinary feature of this case was that Wright had dreamed about the murder on the previous night.'

A cry was torn from Alice; the fringes of her parasol trembled and she turned her face away. McLevy curtailed the story.

Jack looked relieved when it was over. 'A remarkable sermon against strong liquor, Mr McLevy.' He tapped the coachman's arm. 'Pull in at the next likely spot, Andrews.'

They reached Bridge of Garry a minute or so later; the coachman transformed himself into a footman, unpacking the hamper and serving its contents.

When Mrs Vesey offered to join him, Alice said, 'Do not be so silly, Abby! Sit with us.'

Apart from that one remark she was silent throughout the picnic. Jack kept casting watchful looks at her; he appeared well acquainted with her moods.

After half an hour Alice again took control of herself and the expedition. She opened the carriage door.

'Jack, will you take me to the falls?'

He jumped down. 'I'll see to the step, Andrews.' When he helped Alice to the ground Mrs Vesey began to follow.

'You stay there, Abby. I wish to speak to Mr Douglas alone. You must entertain our guest.'

Mrs Vesey said, 'I don't know if I ought.' Her mouth rounded as she suddenly understood what had happened. She flashed an annoyed look at McLevy, then flounced down again.

Jack and Alice walked away into thickets of mountain ash and birch and were soon out of sight.

The coachman uttered a grumbling cough as he stirred on his seat.

'I'll hold the horses for you if you wish to walk,' offered McLevy.

Andrews gave a grateful grin and clambered down from the box. 'Do the same for you, mate, when I get back. Rum and Brandy won't give no trouble.'

McLevy went to the animals' heads and held their bridles.

A vexed mutter came from Mrs Vesey. 'Well, of all the –! I should of known she was up to something. It was downright odd her suggesting you to join us.' She pressed her hand to her mouth. 'Oh, begging your pardon, Mr McLevy!'

He was amused, and diverted their conversation. 'My story seemed to distress Miss Enderby. I am truly sorry.'

'You wasn't to know. I thought she got over them nightmares long ago.'

'Nightmares?'

'When she was sixteen. Terrible time we had with her, for all of six months. Her poor mama went nearly out of her mind.'

'Mr Enderby also would be anxious.'

'He was demented, him doting so. The mistress sent her to Brighton for the winter. Quiet as a ghost, poor lamb. She never really got over it. Her meeting Captain Hatterton was a blessing out of heaven, you might say.'

'Have they been acquainted long?'

Mrs Vesey did some mental calculation. 'It was March

last year they met. Mr Hatterton proposed at Kilcorrie a year ago.' Her expression became tender. 'It's nice having the wedding here, don't you think?'

McLevy led the conversation towards Jack Douglas; he was unsurprised to learn that Jack and Alice had known each other since childhood.

'There *was* talk about them being sweethearts, but it never would do. Even if Mr Douglas hadn't given up his dinners. Between you and me, Mrs Enderby was hoping for a baronet.'

He learned that Jack's father handled all Mr Enderby's financial affairs, and that Jack had broken his mother's heart by throwing over a career at the bar. He had articled himself in his father's office and spent all his spare time working among the undeserving poor. That was Mrs Vesey's phrase. She also told him that Mr Enderby had made his fortune in the brewing industry.

'And what about yourself, Mrs Vesey? Have you been long in the Enderbys' service?'

The response was frosty. 'Not in their *service*, Mr McLevy. More like a companion.'

He apologised, and Mrs Vesey hastened to establish her status.

'Us and the Greenaways was neighbours once. That was before Rose Greenaway changed her name to Enderby. Mr Enderby was only a foreman when he started courting. Rose was parlourmaid to old Mrs Douglas then. *She* was Mr Jack's grandmother.'

After the coachman returned McLevy took a turn in the woods himself, thinking about this intriguing information.

When he reached the falls he saw Alice standing perilously near the edge, with Jack Douglas a few steps behind her. His hands were clenched behind his back. Alice turned round; despite the thunder of water her clear voice reached McLevy.

'How high is the fall, Jack?'

'About eighteen feet, I think. It looks higher because of the width and mass of water.'

'Do you suppose that Miles could leap across? You know how he loves taking wagers.'

'Too dangerous for a bridegroom, Lissie.'

Alice laughed, and they began to saunter away from the river. McLevy withdrew by another route, reaching the carriage before them. Something must have happened in the few minutes they were out of his sight. When he next saw them Jack was frowning, and there was an angry brightness in Alice's eyes.

Had he made a belated attempt to stop the wedding? Perhaps it was something in the Perthshire air. McLevy had never known a place so productive of quarrels.

Chapter Seven

Miles Hatterton's friends had nicknamed him 'Leo' because of his reddish-blond head and languid bulk. Like a lion, he could move out of sloth with unnerving speed while still preserving that unruffled, leonine gaze.

Until his aunt took him up Miles had had little intimate contact with women, apart from some whose social status was too removed from his own to promote introspection. He fell easily into the habits of whatever company he gathered around him; but it was always the same kind of company.

Over the past two years his normal pursuits had lost their appeal. Those who joined in were now ten years his junior. When Mrs Melton suggested that he should find a wife, Miles thought it might be rather jolly to be married. He liked to please his aunt.

His thoughts about Alice were warm but unfocused. He supposed life would go on as usual after their marriage, apart from his having to sell out of the army.

After dinner on Monday night Mr Enderby asked Miles to join him in the library. He waited at the door until he saw his future son-in-law walking across the hanging gallery above the hall. After they were seated he offered Miles a cigar. He puffed his own nervously, perplexed about the best way to break the news.

'Dashed awkward time for you to leave Mrs Melton.'

'Oh, I think she'll be with us for some time yet. I'm sure the old girl won't snuff out before Alice has a chance to meet her.'

They were to visit his aunt on their way to Italy. Mrs Enderby had agreed to let Abby Vesey travel with them during the wedding tour, since Alice would need a lady's maid.

Henry Enderby cleared his throat. 'Didn't want to tell you in front of the ladies. I had a letter from Mrs Melton's solicitor this morning. There's one for you.' He thrust across a black-edged envelope.

Miles held the letter in his hand for a moment before breaking the black seal. He read the contents twice, his head stooped between his shoulders.

'Clark says she had a relapse.'

'Ah, he didn't tell me that. Only that Mrs Melton died on Saturday morning. What a pity you had to leave her to go to Edinburgh. I'm very sorry, Miles.'

'Didn't think she'd go so soon. She was my godmother as well as my aunt.' Miles's head remained bent.

Henry Enderby looked away, giving the young man time to recover himself.

Miles went on, 'The funeral's on Thursday.'

Mr Enderby asked, 'Does that mean we'll have to put off the wedding?'

Miles rose and began to pace round the billiard table with the letter held behind his back.

Mr Enderby enquired hesitantly, 'How soon after the funeral would it be decent …?' He let the question hang, unwilling to confirm a postponement.

Miles's brow furrowed. 'Nine months or a year, I suppose.'

Henry Enderby felt a chill of horror as he thought of his wife's recriminations. Then a bold idea presented itself. Miles had no near relations; his mother was dead, his father an invalid too housebound to attend the wedding. Only a few of his regimental friends would be among the guests.

'Why don't we let it stand? I could hold back the London papers so that no one in Kilcorrie will know. If your friends hear about Mrs Melton's decease you can tell them to keep mum.'

Miles said loftily, 'I prefer not to lie, sir.'

'You're asking a lot, expecting Alice to wait so long. She'll break her heart.'

This reproach produced a flicker of hesitation. The two men looked at each other.

Mr Enderby exclaimed heartily, 'In for a penny, in for a pound. Can't ask all those nobs from Perth to put it off so near the date.'

'I didn't think of that,' said Miles. Mr Enderby felt his anxiety lift a little. 'Charles Clark won't know his letters arrived today. I'll tell him we didn't hear until -'

He backed down before Miles's anger. 'All right. If you'd been in business, m'lad, you wouldn't be so high and mighty about a few fibs.' Had he dared he would have asked Miles to keep Mrs Melton's death from Alice.

Miles stroked his corn-coloured moustache for a moment. 'All right. I'll tell Clark that I can't attend the funeral. He doesn't know the date of the wedding.' He added defiantly, 'I wouldn't do this for anyone except Alice.'

Mr Enderby patted the young man's shoulder. 'I know, Miles. Let's go back to her, shall we?'

As they made their way to the drawing-room, Mr Enderby decided it would be prudent to repeat the conversation to his daughter. He'd say that Miles had been torn between respect for his aunt and his love for Alice. That should avoid any disagreement on the wedding tour.

What he liked best about Miles was his prowess with rod and gun. He had even taken him out stalking, the one sport he never shared with his guests. He would miss Alice after Miles took her off his hands, but he had to admit it would be a relief. Her illness had terrified him; he had always ducked any discussion about it with his wife.

Best not tell Rosie about the aunt's death until the youngsters were spliced. She was upset enough already.

Chapter Eight

On Tuesday morning McLevy told himself he must visit the minister. He had been delaying because of Jeanie's misbehaviour. After breakfast he went upstairs to fetch his hat and coat. In the room was a small, sandy-haired man who was untying a crushed paper parcel.

'It's a wee space for the two of us,' grumbled Jimmy Dewar. He laid out his flannel shirt and nightgown on the undershelf of the wash-stand.

The minister's manse was the last house in the village. The front garden was full of weeds and unpruned gooseberry bushes. A young and very thin servant maid answered McLevy's ring at the bell.

'I'm busy with Mr Bisset's dinner. Go you in to his study.' She pointed to a door at the end of the hall.

The deep, rich voice was intoning beyond it. McLevy knocked, was told to enter, and discovered the minister surrounded by a dozen children to whom he was giving a Scripture reading. Each child was following the text on a beautifully written sheet of paper, evidently the work of the minister. Mr Bisset put down his Bible.

'We'll conclude for the day, bairns.'

McLevy apologised for his untimely visit.

'Not at all, sir. I was about to finish.' Mr Bisset patted the disappearing heads with a smile which became considerably less warm when he turned to his visitor.

McLevy had a liking for handsomeness in both men and women; he could not repress an uncharitable response to Mr Bisset's greasy skin and lank hair. The lips lay slightly apart, disclosing blackened teeth.

However, the minister showed himself tolerant of Jeanie's interruption, saying that canine as well as human flesh was frail.

Once over that obstacle McLevy came to the point. He had noticed a memorial tablet on the church wall; Calum Macdonald, the previous minister, had died in March 1860.

'I need your assistance, sir. I believe you were in charge of the parish during the investigation of the Sanders case.'

'No, I did not arrive until August, after the police had concluded their enquiries. But it was the talk of the district for months afterwards.'

'Who preached in the intervening months?'

'No one.'

'No one?' McLevy was surprised.

Mr Bisset made a hideous grimace. 'You seem unaware that I was imposed on the parish, not called here by the congregation. My arrival was delayed.' He went into pained reminiscence. 'As a result almost the whole congregation gradually deserted to the Free Presbyterian church at Inverconan.'

There might be more to that than religious principle. Mr Bisset's shirt gaped open, and his jacket – black, but not of clerical cut – was food-spattered, while his eyes and hands were in a constant fidget.

'I do not understand, Mr Bisset.' The old minister had been as up in years as Methuselah. Surely there must have been some young probationer eager for his pulpit?

'I formerly acted as tutor to the sons of a gentleman domiciled near Elgin. He was a personal friend of his lordship and leased Kilcorrie from him for two summers before his appointment to our embassy at Constantinople.

On Mr Macdonald's death my patron wrote to the earl recommending me for the vacant charge and his request was granted immediately.'

Constantinople tickled McLevy's memory, but he could not think why.

'Unfortunately I myself was travelling when his lordship wrote to me with the good news of my appointment. I did not hear about it until late July.'

Grantly Carmichael. Of course. There had been a paragraph in the news journals during early summer of that year.

'Was there not a boating accident on the Bosphorus?'

'Alas, yes. He and his wife with my two pupils were drowned a few months after they reached Constantinople.'

The discordance between the suave manner and the outward man was making McLevy uncomfortable; he longed to end the interview.

The minister asked, 'You are from the fair green land of Erin, Mr McLevy?'

'I fared from Ireland more than thirty years past, sir. You are a Highlander, I think.'

'From Argyll. I studied in Glasgow.' He pulled at a loose thread in his cuff. 'I myself was at Kilcorrie with Mr Grantly Carmichael and his family during the summers of 1858 and 1859. The house has been rebuilt since then.'

McLevy was becoming used to Mr Bisset's oblique way of nudging facts towards him. He tilted his eyebrows into a question.

'I accompanied the family to Glencrannich, and Mr Macdonald asked me to help bring his communion and catechising registers up to date. He was almost blind before he died. The records form a memorial of comings and goings in the glen during fifty years. I continued the habit for the few months in which I had a full congregation.'

'Do they include May and June of 1860?'

'Indeed they do, Mr McLevy. I keep the registers in this room.'

'Would a murderer put himself forward in such a way?'

'He would be ill-advised not to, if he wished to escape the scandal of atheism.'

That seemed probable in a country area such as Glencrannich. Mr Bisset had another attack of the fidgets then asked, 'Why do you assume this person has relations in the glen?'

'We brought the thieves together before the committal and told them about the child's death. They had not witnessed the assault, and we hoped to loosen their tongues. Peter Sanders had nothing useful to say. It was the woman who informed us that their accomplice was shortly to return to his folk in Glencrannich. Apparently he told them so before they planned the robbery. He must have sweated at his indiscretion.'

'And so was less likely to return here, Mr McLevy.'

'I would stake my life that he was in your church on Sunday morning. My dog smelt him. That was why she growled.'

Yet like so many who had wanted to see the bride the man could have been drawn in by mere curiosity and not be a regular worshipper. It was hard to tell whether Mr Bisset was gurgling in disbelief or trying to repress a laugh. His tongue curved round the discoloured teeth. 'Is that all? You place great trust in a woman's word. Did you question those miscreants again?'

'There was little opportunity. She died in the Infirmary that summer, eaten up with clap. The man was sent to Perth for hard labour. A few days later he hanged himself in his cell. He had learned that the child was his brother's daughter.'

The minister rose to his feet so quickly that a sheaf of papers was swept off his desk. He stood for some moments, then took out a grubby handkerchief and blew his nose. The words came out in a choked whisper.

'Two human souls destroyed as well as the child! Forgive me, Mr McLevy. As a student I worked in the city missions, but one forgets such evils exist, in this – this peaceful retreat...'

McLevy got to his feet. 'Perhaps within a few days you will allow me to inspect those lists.'

Mr Bisset bobbed his head in agreement, and McLevy left him. It occurred to him that the minister might suffer from some form of palsy, but if so, would his hand be steady enough to produce that beautiful calligraphy?

When he was alone, David Bisset returned to his desk. He uncapped the ink bottle and sat nibbling the end of a goose-feather pen. After a few moments he bounded to his feet and opened a cupboard out of which he took a large earthenware bottle and a glass. He poured half a pint of whisky, half of which he gulped off before sitting down with the glass beside him.

The second hateful visit that day. The first had been Hector McIver's.

He suspected that Hector attended the parish church only to remind him that he was a usurper; Mr Macdonald had always hoped his favourite pupil would succeed him.

Hector had lowered himself into a chair without invitation.

'I want your word to Mr Enderby.'

'For Donald? I thought it was settled that he is to have Rob Brodie's place in March. You must speak to Mr Ogg about his marriage.' The other McIvers attended the Free Church at Inverconan.

'It is about the laird taking back my lease in May.'

'I am grieved, but can do nothing about it, Mr McIver.'

Hector stood up and banged the minister's desk. 'Johnnie Itchbag stole my grandfather's house and made him walk ten miles to work the croft. Just that the Itchbag could put his hure near the big house!'

Mr Bisset recalled that 'Johnnie Itchbag' was a previous

Lord Dunfillan, and the 'hure' a mistress who had been disposed of when the earl married. This gossip was twenty years old.

'Did your father not receive back the house?'

'What is the use of that when Mr Enderby is driving us out of the glen?'

Although he disliked Hector, Mr Bisset was moved by this howl of anguish. He imagined the four McIver children tugging at the shafts of their peat-cart as they plodded barefoot to Dunfillan. The cart was piled with a few blankets, rusty pots and pans, and one squawking hen. The picture was so vivid that he started when Hector spoke again.

'Ach, Calum Macdonald was a better man than you! He did not lick the laird's boots or have me correct his Gaelic sermons. Will you help or no?'

David Bisset pulled himself together. 'Your request is preposterous. How can I meddle with estate business? Now, please leave. It is time for my Bible scholars.'

Hector edged the chair closer to David Bisset's desk; his voice softened into menace. 'I think you *will* put a word for me to the laird.'

The minister's thoughts flew to his college days in Glasgow when he had conducted a short liaison with a woman who claimed he had made her pregnant. He was sending money to her mother twice a year. Surely Hector could not know about that?

'There's speak about yon whisky still up the glen, and what they give you to help them dodge the gaugers. If you do not help me with the laird I will be reporting you to the excise office. You'll never live fifty years with us like Mr Macdonald, and maybe Mr Enderby will not live at all.'

Terror swept through Mr Bisset, and his forehead beaded with sweat. Eventually he would think of a way to outwit Hector; at the moment he needed to stave off his threat. He adopted a conciliating tone. 'There is some justice in your argument, Mr McIver. I shall remind Mr Enderby that you have a young family to support.'

'You will be sensible. That is good.'

Contempt for Hector's gullibility mingled with his own relief. 'It would be useless to approach the laird this week. Can we not let the wedding go by?'

'Certainly, Mr Bisset. I'll be back to you on Friday.'

Only after his tormentor had left did David Bisset realise that Hector had also threatened Mr Enderby.

Chapter Nine

Rose Enderby's anger still simmered, but she was forced to give most of her attention to the commissariat of provisions arriving for the wedding. Everything was conveyed by train to Dunfillan and from there by carriers' wagons to Kilcorrie, where the items had to be labelled and stored. The more bulky arrived trussed in cheesecloth or packed in straw. The confectioner who had made the wedding cake escorted it into the pantry. A special cart delivered a dozen boxes of fireworks, marked in red paint.

The family guests were expected on Tuesday; on Wednesday a team of workmen would erect the marquee for the wedding breakfast.

From time to time, Mrs Enderby paused to consider her grievance. It was growing to monstrous size.

Attack was the best defence, Jimmy Dewar decided. On Tuesday evening he asked Mary to draw him some ale, and then walked across the taproom to sit beside the Edinburgh policeman. He had not turned up for work on Monday, having almost decided not to return to the glen at all. The thought of all the free hospitality at the wedding had brought him back. That and Isa's nagging. She'd gone on and on. Sometimes he felt like splitting her tongue with a chisel.

He said, 'What a waste of all yon gear at Bealach nan

Bo.' This was the name of the mountain pass through which the deer were to be driven for the tinchel.

'What are you and the others doing up there, Mr Dewar?'

'Mending two hundred yards of dyke, then we're to set posts and wire on top, so the deer'll no get away frae the guns. All for a few hours' sport! It's fine to be gentry, eh?'

The policeman smiled. He was a big-built chap with a strong Irish brogue. Lazy-looking, Jimmy thought.

He went on, 'The gillies get a bottle of whisky and half a crown each. No me, though.'

'Are you not going to the tenants' dinner?'

'Oh, aye, everybody gets to that.'

The dinner was to be held in the peat shed of the home farm at the rear of the ruined Corrie Castle. Mr Enderby had put in a plank floor; generous quantities of food and drink would be supplied by the estate.

Jimmy wondered if the peeler had been asked by the laird to find out what the McIvers were up to. Maybe he was sniffing after those candlesticks he'd nabbed from Skellie Castle. He tried the McIvers first. He remarked with a suggestive grin, 'Yon Janet McIver's a bonny lass.'

'I do not know her.'

'A pity she's no got a man of her own. She's a bittie old, but she'd still be a fine armful, eh?' Seeing the policeman's expression he added quickly, 'No for me, mind. I'm a married man myself.'

Jimmy couldn't think how to bring up the subject of Skellie Castle, so he returned to the Enderbys. 'There's queer on-goings at the big house.'

'H'mn.' The big Irishman sat back and took out his pipe.

'I was in the kitchen at my supper. They make you eat the same time as the gentry.

'H'mn,' said the peeler again, seeming only half interested.

'There's been an awfy carry-on with the laird's wife and yon English body she brought frae London screeching one at the other. Mistress Frazer was telling the cook about it. She's the housekeeper. I heard the two of them talking in a room off the kitchen, but no the end of it. She banged the door shut.'

The policeman gave a sleepy smile. 'Great folk have their problems the same as us.'

Just a poor old soul working out his term, Jimmy decided. Likely they'd sent him about that whisky still the Kilcorrie servant lassies said was up the glen.

'It seems so heartless to proceed with the wedding,' said Alice. She had been told by Miles about his aunt's death. 'You will want to attend Mrs Melton's funeral.'

They had managed to find a corner to themselves in the crowded drawing-room. It was the day before the wedding.

'I agree it isn't quite the thing but you surely don't want us to cry off? Your pater wouldn't have it. Said you'd break your heart. That settled it for me.'

Alice blushed. 'You silly, dear boy!'

'There's something else.' Miles stretched out his right foot and frowned at it for a moment. 'The old girl died still swearing blind about my birthday.'

'Dearest, I hope you told Mr Clark the truth. It would have been rather foolish not to, when you knew that Mrs Melton might – might never recover.'

'No, I didn't.'

Alice said, 'You do not need to humour *that* whim any longer. Write to him.'

'It seems so disloyal, the moment the old girl's dead. What difference does it make? It's only a day out.'

Alice curled her hand round Miles's sleeve.

'You are perfection, my darling, but sometimes I wish you were not so willing to please other people.'

'Why not, if there's no harm in it? I'm a real demon

once I make up my mind. Like that ferret.'

Alice's smile faltered. 'I'd rather you hadn't told me that story, beloved. Why are schoolboys so barbaric?'

'So that angels like you may reform us, my darling.'

Mrs Enderby walked across to them and put her hand on Alice's shoulder. 'I claim a mother's final privilege, Miles. I should like to speak to Alice alone.'

Mrs Enderby was usually exhilarated by the challenge of organisation, but the last few days had depressed and exhausted her. In addition, her husband had flown into a rage when she suggested that they ought to tell Miles about Alice's illness.

She had intended to speak to her daughter about wifely duty; over the past two years she had noticed alarming signs of strong-mindedness in Alice. Once they reached her private parlour anxiety made her plunge straight into her main concern.

'Have you yet spoken to Papa about leasing Kilcorrie to Miles?'

A flush rose to Alice's cheeks. 'Why, no, Mama. I have not had the opportunity.'

'There will be even less time tomorrow!'

'It is such a private matter. We would have to speak alone.'

Mrs Enderby thought she must have misheard. 'Whenever I see you and Papa together you are laughing over some secret. May you not for once have a serious conversation?'

Her daughter looked acutely distressed. Mrs Enderby wondered how long Alice had been aware of this cause of disagreement between her parents.

'We must make the opportunity for you to speak to him,' she said decisively. 'I shall send Papa to you.' She left the room.

Alice remained in Mrs Enderby's parlour, waiting for her father. She went to stand on the left side of the hearthrug, holding her crinoline away from the firescreen. The gilt mirror above the mantelpiece was divided by three slender pilasters; it reflected back her head and bare shoulders.

Why was it so hard to tell Papa that she wanted him to give Kilcorrie to Miles? She wished Mama wouldn't be so insistent.

Mama had already warned Alice that she would feel sad at leaving Papa. That was the way things happened when girls were married. The regret would pass. Imagine, Mama had said, having to choose between two delicious boxes of chocolate.

It wasn't like that at all. Alice woke herself at nights with wild sobbing. When she looked at her left hand and imagined herself wearing a wedding ring, there was dread mingled with her pleasure. She wouldn't feel safely married until she and Miles were on their way to Italy. Since meeting him last March, she had found it difficult to kiss Papa. She didn't understand this, nor why she felt such anguish when she was placed between them at dinner.

Alice glanced round at the door. She had not been alone with Papa for four years.

The thought rose with startling precision. She and Papa often joked together in the drawing-room after dinner, in whispers; they drove in Hyde Park without Mama; but for four years they had never been together in a place where nobody else could see them.

Alice sat down, and placed her hands in her lap. They were chilled and trembling.

Mr Enderby walked into the room. 'My dear little lovebird!'

He went across to the brass fender and stood facing his daughter with an air of expectancy, his hands lifting his coat tails.

'What do you wish to tell Papa?'

Alice found she couldn't meet her father's eyes. Had

Mama already told him what she would say? Then Papa's jovial manner must mean he really did intend to give Kilcorrie to Miles. Alice had begun to feel some doubts about this.

'Papa, when Miles and I return from Italy -'

'My little girl will be a married lady with her own establishment. Think of that!'

'Yes, but where, Papa? Must it be London?'

Henry Enderby began to pick up the ornaments on the mantelpiece. 'Don't you wish to be near Mama and me?' His voice was humorously indignant.

'Miles will become restless if he has no occupation.'

'Don't I know that, my precious! I've plans for your husband to work in the City. He shall travel by train from Bucksteads two or three times a week... Shouldn't I discuss this with Miles, not with Papa's little mouse?'

'Miles would like to live at Kilcorrie, Papa, and so should I.'

From the startled look on his face she was convinced that the whole idea was her mother's. With this realisation came another: it would be exciting to make Papa give in to her.

Mr Enderby walked around the room, tapping each piece of furniture as he passed it. 'That's a facer, Alice, a real facer.' At last, shaking his head like a dog emerging from water, he halted in front of her. 'Tell you what, I'll let Miles have the lease next spring, after you come back from Italy. How's that? Keep it to yourself, there's a good little girl.'

'Can't I tell Miles?'

Mr Enderby took out his cigar case. His hands plucked twice at the clasp before he could open it.

'Yes, of course. I meant your mother.'

Alice stood up and forced herself to kiss her father on the forehead. As he backed away she saw tears in his eyes.

'Tell Mama I'm going to the library for a smoke. Be

over soon.' He left hurriedly.

Alice was astonished at her easy victory. Papa had not wanted to give away Kilcorrie! Yet that didn't explain his tears. A sense of elation filled her, mingled with a rather pleasant kind of grief.

She stared at herself in the mirror. Not visibly connected with its body, the right hand of her reflection rose into view and touched a side ringlet. She began to shiver although she felt hot inside. It was like cool air stroking one's skin on a summer's day. She sat down by the fireside.

'Be over soon,' she said, huddling over her knees.

This was the last occasion on which Henry and Alice Enderby spoke to each other.

Chapter Ten

When David Bisset remembered it was Thursday, he sat up and thrust back the bedclothes. After he had washed and shaved, he ran to the top of the stairs.

'My bands, did you starch them?'

Jenny shouted from below, 'Aye, and there's a clean shirt airing by the fire.'

After donning a full set of clerical garments he rushed to the kitchen, where he hastily consumed porridge and tea.

Jenny wrinkled her nose. 'Fegs, the stink of camphor on yon coat!'

Mr Bisset pushed by her to stand in the porch. A vehicle had been promised to take him to Kilcorrie at half past eight.

He waited five minutes before it arrived. It was a flawless late summer's day; the early mist had lifted and there were a only few ripples of cirrus streaking the blue. Mr Bisset felt pleased with himself; not once had he reached for the whisky jar. For the next few hours he would be mixing with his equals, as in those palmy days with the Grantly Carmichaels.

As he rode beside the silent groom his tranquillity began to give way to gloom, and he felt the weight of an immense weariness. He had hardly slept during the past two nights. Had his Christian conscience allowed it, he thought, there were at least three people he could have wished dead that morning.

At Kilcorrie House Mrs Enderby and Abby Vesey were helping Alice into her wedding gown. Their quarrel had been suspended in a mutual wish not to spoil her day. In the next room Miles was being inspected by a friend from the regiment out of which he had sold in July. The groomsman looked on critically as Miles circled before the mirror in his dress uniform. He himself was in civilian dress.

'Seeing you ain't a plunger any more, old Leo, should you go full fig?'

'It's the last time, Charlie. Just to please the dear girl.'

Charlie wriggled on his lavender gloves and followed Miles to the drawing-room with a disapproving frown.

They arrived at the same time as Mr Bisset and Mrs Enderby. The house guests were half hidden behind the mass of roses and lilies that covered every surface. Champagne and cake were set out on a buffet table, but the servants who were to hand them around had been told to wait outside in the corridor.

Alice arrived a few minutes later on her father's arm. She smiled at the group awaiting her. Mr Bisset stepped forward, and Mr Enderby nodded at the butler, who retreated through the doors and closed them.

McLevy was picked up by the Balinmore dogcart. He had overcome his doubts about accompanying the McLarens to the wedding breakfast. Dr Sandy pointed to the stout leather portmanteau strapped beside him. 'Flora's confounded folderols.'

His sister retorted, 'Sandy, even you do not intend to present yourself at the ball in a shooting jacket and those old sit-upons.'

She explained that Mrs Enderby had set aside some rooms in which the day guests might change for the ball. 'Of course, there will be many who will arrive only after the tinchel.'

'A most ingenious fudge,' commented her brother. Flora flashed him a warning look, and this remark was not expanded.

From the Kilcorrie gates McLevy caught sight of a canvas marquee fluttering with blue and scarlet pennants. The guests were sauntering between the rose-beds, waiting for the wedding party to emerge from the house.

Dr Sandy drove past a roped enclosure on which were converging the estate tenants and their families. There was already a long queue at a barrel where some liquor was being ladled out.

After handing over the dogcart at the stables, Dr Sandy took his sister and McLevy to join the guests now entering the marquee. Despite the carpet laid over the grass the atmosphere inside was warmly humid. It seemed impossible that the crowded space would hold them all; then an unseen band struck up, and everyone settled down at the tables. Among a jungle of flowers and ferns were spread jellies, cold fish, poultry, sweet and savoury tartlets, game pies and salads. The bridal cake out-topped all the other items.

McLevy had a good view of Mr and Mrs Enderby; he saw Alice when she stood up to place her bouquet among the marguerites and maidenhair on the top tier of the cake. She pierced it with her bridegroom's sword, which Miles then re-sheathed and handed, baldric and all, to his groomsman.

Beyond the novelty of attending a society wedding there was little to interest McLevy. He was more familiar with impromptu penny bridals in Edinburgh's Royal Mile; and his presence there usually resulted in a lengthy separation of bride and groom. He applied himself to the lavish wedding breakfast; after these few days his appetite as well as his hearing had improved. He was amused to see that Flora made a much heartier meal than her brother.

As Jack Douglas rose to propose the bride's health, his hand gripped tightly round his glass, McLevy began to realise that several things were amiss. Alice's parents were sitting at opposite ends of the main table. Mrs Enderby became visibly agitated when her husband stood up to praise their son-in-law. Two journalists were placed at a small side-table to McLevy's left. As they uncapped their ink-pots they exchanged knowing smiles; but the speech seemed to surprise them.

Mrs Enderby's face was now glassed over by a rigid smile, carefully ignored by her husband. Other speeches followed, and then the guests began to move around; a little later they were drifting out of the marquee. McLevy watched the Enderbys; he wondered if the signs of their obscure battle were as clear to the other guests.

He went over to the newspapermen. They had put up their reports and one was edging towards the crumbs of broken icing round the bridal cake.

'We expected him to give Captain Hatterton the lease of Kilcorrie,' he explained. 'Mrs Enderby would dearly like to cry off her Highland holidays.' His companion nodded while gobbling a plateful of apples *à la Parisienne*.

'You are clairvoyant, sir?'

The man grinned. 'Merely well informed by a friend in the estate factor's office at Dunfillan.'

McLevy rejoined the McLarens, meaning to thank them and say goodbye.

Dr Sandy cried out, 'You can't go now, man! You must watch the running of the deer.'

A sharp glance from Flora lighted first on her brother and then on the detective.

'Mr McLevy is anxious about his dog, Sandy. She is confined in the Dunfillan Arms and needs to walk.'

'Is she a biddable beast?'

'For me, Jeanie Brash would hop all the way up a hill on one paw!' Mr McLevy wished truth upon the lie with two fingers crossed behind his back.

'Let's drive down to collect her.'

'I shall walk, Dr McLaren. It is of no consequence if I miss the tinchel.'

'Nonsense! We don't set out for another hour. Let's divide our togs, Flora.'

'Perhaps Mr McLevy would find a servant lass to whom I may pass my gown.'

She walked towards the stables, obviously confident that her request would be obeyed. McLevy re-entered the marquee. A dozen servants were clearing the tables under the supervision of a grey-haired woman in an apron.

McLevy spoke to her, and she gave some orders to a maidservant. On his way out he noticed Jack Douglas still sitting at table with two champagne bottles in front of him.

Before McLevy could reach the entrance his name was called out. He turned round unwillingly. Though sorry for the young man he despised his self-indulgence.

'That's that, then.' The words stumbled out thickly.

'Come, come, Mr Douglas. No man grows old without losing a sweetheart or two. You must take your share with the rest of us.'

'Shouldn't let her marry without telling, McLevy. Could kill him!'

McLevy prised the bottle out of Jack's hand and set it out of reach. 'I suppose the young lady has been free to choose.'

He had credited Jack Douglas with more bottom.

Dr Sandy was waiting at the stables. From another outbuilding came the sad, eerie howling of deerhounds.

'How many beasts do you expect to kill?' asked McLevy as the pony trotted towards the village.

'I have no idea. There hasn't been a tinchel round here since the Battle of the Bannockstone.'

After surviving this medieval blood feast a Balinmore

ancestor had composed a song about it in Gaelic. Dr Sandy's translation occupied the rest of their drive to the Dunfillan Arms.

Jeanie Brash was tied by the stable pump, from where she was keeping an eye on the scavenging hens. McLevy untied her leash from the iron ring and let her run around. Approaching the kitchen, he heard Dr Sandy say, 'I'll be over not long after midnight.'

They were on their way back to the dogcart when Mrs Gregory came running after them.

'Balinmore, there's a letter for Captain Hatterton. I was going to send it by Ritchie.'

Dr Sandy held out his hand and then looked at the envelope. 'This hasn't been posted.'

'No, it's from a gentleman who has just arrived.'

'Perhaps I had better meet him, Isobel. He may wish to send a message as well as the letter.'

McLevy returned to the dogcart with Jeanie Brash, and after five minutes Dr Sandy joined him.

'A man named Charles Clark,' he explained as they returned to Kilcorrie. 'He's the solicitor who does for young Hatterton's aunt. She's supposed to be leaving him a fortune when she dies. I wonder why he's turned up in Glencrannich.'

Chapter Eleven

The older women settled on the garden benches in the shade of their parasols. Under Alice's leadership – 'Why should the gentlemen have all the sport?' – an archery target was set up for those young and active enough to compete.

Some of the men stayed behind to watch them, but all who considered themselves sportsmen went to change into shooting dress.

'It's an hour's walking to Bealach nan Bo, gentlemen,' said Brodie. A fit pair of legs could reach the dykes in forty minutes but some would find it a hard trudge.

While the workmen sat on the balustrade waiting to let down the marquee, the Kilcorrie servants removed the tables and the food left over from the wedding breakfast.

Jimmy Dewar had been idling in the ginger beer enclosure all morning, but now he edged towards the house. He managed up the stair no bother at all; there he nicked a couple of rings and a silver-mounted comb before an old body in black bombazine asked what he thought he was up to. Jimmy explained he had lost his way, and retreated to the park. Unchancy to hang around the house any longer. He'd toddle back to the village and wait for the tenants' dinner.

Henry Enderby heard the sound of a window being opened in his wife's bedroom. Slipping on the braces of his tweed knickerbockers, he went into it and found Mrs Enderby with her arms akimbo on the windowsill, looking up the glen. 'Rosie, you should ring for a servant to do that.' She remained with her back to him. He moistened his lips. 'Wouldn't you like to walk with the other ladies to the bothy?'

Mrs Enderby turned round. 'You didn't say you were going to hand over Kilcorrie.'

He ran a finger round the inside of his starched collar. 'It wasn't appropriate.' More quickly than he liked he blurted out, 'I did what you wanted. I've promised Alice that Miles can have the estate.'

Her face was pale. 'Why didn't you let me know?'

'Alice can tell Miles herself. That's enough for the moment, isn't it?'

'No! You must speak to Miles before the tinchel.'

Mr Enderby's eyes hunted round the room like a cornered animal. 'I mustn't let them go off without me. For goodness sake, let up, Rosie. It's Alice's wedding day!'

She began to shout and beat her fists on his chest. He easily pushed her away, but the stream of recrimination dropped into his stomach like acid. Eventually he could bear it no longer. He heard her scream as he walked out.

Escaping from the powdery scents of his wife's bedchamber he hurried to the gun room, ashamed of the way he had let her frighten him. He knew she had set Alice on and took some spiteful consolation from the thought that she had been tormenting herself needlessly.

Their quarrels were never so destructive in London. In the dark warmth of the marital bed they would struggle to some compromise. There he found the threat of her temper exciting.

The gun room was full of men stuffing their pockets with cartridges and making a final inspection of guns.

Donald McIver was giving assistance to those who needed it. There was a smell of oil and well-polished leather.

Mr Enderby lifted his favourite Purdey from the rack. As he filled his ammunition pouch he felt calmer. The fragrance of pipe and cigar smoke drifted through the door; he was uplifted by a sense of male camaraderie.

What could she do except rant and rave? Poor Rosie. Mr Enderby felt magnanimous. He'd speak to Miles, just to appease her. Nothing too final or binding, though. Despite that promise to Alice he wasn't going to hand over his estate before it suited him.

The shooting party waited for their host in the cobbled yard behind the house. Six or seven gillies were grouped near the deer larder. Through the open gate McLevy caught sight of the ponies plodding in single file along the edge of the wood.

He and several other men were standing beside a dozen women who intended to watch the tinchel. Miss McLaren was to join the guns. Dr Sandy laughed aloud at McLevy's amazement.

'Flora's going to Glenquoich in October to stalk with another Amazon.' He looked around and demanded testily, 'Where's Enderby got to? It's a quarter past two. We'll miss the run.'

Donald McIver stepped out of the doorway and called to one of the gillies, 'You'll mind to take thae two brutes up to the dykes, Will?'

'Oh, aye.' The man went to the kennels and returned hanging on to the leashes of the deerhounds.

A few moments later Henry Enderby emerged from the back door. The shooting party turned towards him.

'Have you seen Captain Hatterton, Brodie?'

The gamekeeper replied that he thought Miles had gone to look for Mrs Hatterton. The guests began to stir impatiently.

At that moment Abby Vesey ran out of the back door and made urgent signals. Mr Enderby affected not to see her until his guests began to stare and whisper. With an irritated mutter he handed his gun to the gamekeeper and walked over.

McLevy's curiosity was aroused by the dumbshow of their meeting. At first Henry Enderby returned only curt nods. Then his manner changed: he seemed to catch Mrs Vesey's alarm and began to question her. Between answers she bit the back of her hand in melodramatic despair.

After a few more exchanges Mr Enderby grasped Abby's arm and pushed her out of sight through the back door. He returned to his guests a few moments later.

'Silly woman!' He was laughing in a forced manner.

'There is nothing wrong, I hope?'

'Not at all, Miss McLaren. A small domestic crisis.' He held out a hand for his gun. 'Brodie, you lead our party up to the dykes. I'll wait for Captain Hatterton.'

He stared unseeingly as the party trooped through the gate into the parkland.

The news, whatever it had been, was going to ruin his shooting, thought McLevy. Mr Enderby held his gun wedged under his right arm; the hands thrust into his pockets were shaking uncontrollably.

Miles Hatterton bounded out of the doorway. 'Sorry, sir, I had to have a word with Alice.'

Mr Enderby was on the point of saying that Miles had the rest of his life to have a word with Alice; but instead he felt a rush of terror, remembering the conversation with Abby Vesey.

Miles said, 'That fellow Clark has come down from York on the overnight mail.'

'Damn! Never mind, he won't know his letters arrived on Monday... Hurry up, Miles, we have to overtake the others.'

'What about Clark?'

'Ask him to join us this evening.'

'Is that necessary, sir? He only wants to see me about signing some papers. I could go down to the village now and finish the business.'

'You would miss the tinchel. We'll find a way to bluff it out... Do come on!'

Henry Enderby walked to the gate, nerving himself for what he must say to Miles before they joined the sporting party. His son-in-law followed him. Mr Enderby stopped and turned round.

'Look here, Miles, there's something I have to tell you.'

He must thrust aside his own humiliation. The important thing was Alice's happiness. After the first terrible words he did not find it difficult. Miles listened intently, with a serious look on his face. Underneath that schoolboy lingo he was an astute fellow.

'Dashed generous of you, sir,' he said finally. 'I'm sure we can make the arrangement work.'

Henry Enderby strode forward in buoyant relief. Now he could enjoy the tinchel. 'That's the subject closed, then.'

'I'd better dash off a note to Clark,' said Miles. 'Is it all right if I catch you up?'

'I'll wait for you by the beech tree.'

Halfway along the track at the edge of the woods was a clearing with an old beech at its centre. If he was alone, Henry Enderby always stopped here for solemn recollection.

Early frost and snow had presaged that memorably harsh winter of 1860. This was his first visit to Kilcorrie which he had rented for the season. On his usual early morning walk, in mid-October, when he had finally decided to give in to his wife's wish to return to London, he thought he saw poachers in his wood. The trees were bare enough to reveal a flash of movement, but his view was blurred. He went in pursuit of the keeper, then a local man, and told him to bring along his spy glass.

Mr Enderby was informed that the 'poachers' were deer leaving the hills in search of food.

He smiled now, remembering how green he'd been four years ago.

The lad had commented, 'They're early down, sir. I've never kent deer this length into the policies before the New Year.'

'Where do they come from?'

The youth waved a hand vaguely westwards. The deer were the laird's, if he had a notion to shoot them.

Mr Enderby's fancy was hotly gripped. He saw himself nailing up ten-pointer heads and dispatching haunches of venison to his friends in England.

Dropping on one knee the keeper again directed his spy glass into the misty wood. 'There's a passable beast at the back.' They were roe deer, not red, but he did not think the laird would know the difference, nor realise that it was unusual to see them gathered together in such a large group.

Not a stalker himself, he had talked to men who had been up the hill, and he suggested scattering hay in the park. Although the animals were by no means starving they were lured out of the trees by such easy fodder.

Mr Enderby's first unsporting ambush was a disaster. He routed the whole herd when his shoe cracked a frosty twig. The keeper said they should leave the beasts alone while a trail of hay was extended to the open hillside. Mr Enderby, already in the grip of his obsession, refused to leave Kilcorrie.

Because of the bleak weather, their guests had already departed. The old tower-house, still not reconstructed, was draughty and miserably inconvenient. Mrs Enderby and Alice huddled over a peat fire in the shabby drawing-room. Only the kitchen staff managed to keep warm.

A week after their first sighting, the deer were enticed

back to the clearing. The next day the bait was laid past the gardener's cottage, in one side of which an extra window had been cut on Mr Enderby's orders. Below it squatted the keeper and Mr Enderby with three dogs lying beside them. The animals were uttering low, unhappy whines.

Two hinds were killed on the spot; another ran out of sight but was traced to the place where she dropped by splashes of blood on the leaves. Both bucks got away with the rest of the herd.

The young keeper squatted down to bleed and gralloch the carcases, and Mr Enderby insisted on helping. He felt a pungent thrill as he whetted his knife, which was increased by the odours that soon met his nose. As well as he could he followed the keeper's instructions. His cold hands were gloved with heat when he plunged them into the entrails.

That was how his obsession began. Mr Enderby remembered being so overwrought that he had hacked off the head from one of the does and run with it into the house. He was too impatient to wait for the pony cart on which the keeper brought home the other carcases.

The next week he had escorted Rosie and Alice back to London and a fortnight later travelled north again to buy Kilcorrie.

The young keeper left the glen when he heard that Mr Enderby had returned to buy Kilcorrie. Before he went he protested that he had acted under orders: the laird ignored his warning that the pregnant hinds were out of season. Mr Enderby claimed that the keeper misinformed him. For some time afterwards the county gossiped unkindly about 'hedge popping'.

That early kill had been too impulsive. He had made a fool of himself. Nowadays he acted more coolly, although underneath he was bubbling with joy. From the first sight of a head to blooding the carcase there was nothing to beat a good day's stalking. His friends were welcome to the other game, but he never took them up to the deer.

If only he could share that delight with Alice and Rosie! His wedding gift to Alice was not the financial settlement, nor the services of china and crystal chosen by her mother, not even the half-promised lease on Kilcorrie; it was to be the tinchel, to which he had invited a hundred guests. He was sacrificing his deer.

Mr Enderby walked to the edge of the clearing, and glanced back along the track. The shooting party was now beyond the wood and straggling up the hillside towards the dykes.

He must stop thinking about that dreadful conversation with Abby Vesey. Soon he'd be crouched down in the heather waiting for the horizon to break into flowing lines of deer.

Chapter Twelve

At half past three the ladies sank down on the heather, overcome by heat. Like a bumblebee in a garden McLevy was surrounded by flowery undulations of tarlatan and muslin.

'This will never do,' said Flora severely. 'If you remain here the deer will not run past us.' The sun twinkled off the gun barrel crooked over her arm.

The ladies sighed and rose to face the steep remainder of their walk.

The bothy they were making for was a ruined hut overlooking the throat of the pass. The deer ponies had been tethered in the shade of its back wall, while some bracken thrown over the charred rafters protected the guests. Picnic baskets and stools had been put inside the bothy, and two brass tea-kettles were already humming on a turf fire.

After half an hour Jeanie Brash pricked up her ears. A moment later there were distant yelps as the gillies and their dogs tightened the cordon. When the barking and human cries increased, Jeanie stood erect, her back legs stiffened and quivering; McLevy distracted her with a currant scone. He tied her to a bench before going outside.

Below him the sportsmen were crouched behind one of the dykes. In the notch of the pass the colour of the sky had changed to silky grey. The air was as stifling as a city street in July; there would be a storm by evening.

'I hear them approaching, ladies.'

The picnic party crowded into the doorway. Some of the women stood along the outer wall, clutching each other's hands in excitement.

There was a flattened, drumming sound further up the pass; through the haze three deer ran into sight along the dried mud of the track. Then behind them, in rising billows of dust, the mass of the herd jumbled and slithered towards the guns, flanked by a few recklessly leaping dogs.

In such confusion it was hard to tell how many of the shots went home. McLevy saw some of the deer stagger a few yards before falling; others lurched out of sight. Two hinds leapt over the fence and made for the bothy. As the animals trotted towards them two of the women rushed inside.

Luck on their hides, thought McLevy, when the hinds had wheeled back to the safety of the hill.

'Two more harts!' cried the man beside him, as the herd thinned out. The billows of dust were settling. There was another fusillade of shots. Both animals bounced into the air, and fell.

'Is that all?' said one of the women as she emerged through the doorway.

Apparently it was. After such elaborate preparation the slaughter had been concentrated into those brief minutes. When the dust and smoke cleared McLevy counted six deer on the ground. For a few moments two dogs jerked beside them.

There was a period of silence. Walking up to the wall, the shooters edged through a narrow gap to inspect their bag. McLevy noticed a moment of sharp discussion between Mr Enderby and Miles Hatterton; then the two staghounds were uncoupled to run after the wounded deer.

McLevy's companion said that the survivors would stream into the parkland and from there make their way back through the woods.

'Enderby should have put some guns nearer the house,' he observed regretfully, as the picnic party walked over to the dykes. 'He could have headed off another half-dozen.'

Miles went striding after the staghounds. Mr Enderby advanced to meet the spectators, waving triumphantly. He addressed the man who had spoken to McLevy.

'Sutherland, will you take the ladies home?'

'May we not see the ponies being loaded and walk back with them?'

'No, if you please, Mrs Sinclair. It is a messy business, and I'm sending them home by the short cut over the hill.'

They had to pass the carcases on their way down the track. McLevy covered his nose with a handkerchief; a powerful stench was tainting the honey scent of the moor. When the gillies came to gralloch the deer they would find that the stampeding herd had begun their work for them. They had disembowelled their dead.

Chapter Thirteen

At six o'clock the sky was breathing heat from a low grey mantle of cloud. Dr Sandy drove McLevy back to the Dunfillan Arms.

McLevy changed into a clean shirt, and after eating his meal as usual with Mary and the landlady he whistled Jeanie Brash outside. They sauntered past the church, going a mile or so towards Dunfillan. The road was quiet, unlike the village street, which was already crowded with people idling towards the peat house for the tenants' dinner. The carriages bringing guests to the ball would not roll past for another two hours.

He encountered the mason as he returned to the village, and Jeanie switched to McLevy's other side. She was sensitive to dislike.

'Not waiting for the festivities, Mr Dewar?'

The mason had changed out of his working clothes but his boots were muddy. He had his tool-bag in his right hand and the paper-wrapped parcel clutched in the other.

'I'm away to Dunfillan. It's a long road home.' He was walking as fast as he could without breaking into a run.

McLevy seated himself for a smoke on a bench outside the inn stables. It was not quite eight o'clock; he would wait until the fun was fizzing before going to the peat house. He wondered why Jimmy Dewar was giving up a night of free entertainment when his conversation centred almost entirely on food and drink.

When the bird's eye tobacco was glowing in the twilight, McLevy took a letter out of his pocket. It had been waiting for him when he returned from the tinchel. It contained mostly domestic news, but there was one paragraph he wanted to read again.

Tell James he was known as 'Genty Geordie'. They used to laugh at his side-buttoned waistcoat. They were not precisely his folk in Glencrannich.

This had been said to Mary by one of McLevy's former colleagues in the police office. He had recently spoken with a ticket-of-leave man who had known Peter Sanders during his week at Perth.

Genty meant from a better social cut than Peter Sanders's cronies. A failed gambler, perhaps. McLevy had locked up several. But *not precisely his folk*? His sister would have quoted exactly; no point in writing for an explanation. He might have to question her informant.

McLevy's thoughts were interrupted by boisterous laughter behind him. The stable lad walked past swinging two iron buckets.

'Queer folk, the gentry.' He went clanking into the kitchen and returned with the buckets full of steaming water.

McLevy went to take a look. Under the lantern four naked young men stood round the horse-trough, glistening with soapsuds. They were scrubbing each other's backs and taking turns to plunge into the trough. A face turned towards him and grinned; its owner waved a dripping arm. Captain Hatterton jumped out and seized a towel.

McLevy remembered the McLarens saying that the male guests were to be provided with hot baths after their vigorous day. They would be driven to temporary billets among the tenantry up and down the glen.

Luxury depended on a sense of occasion, he decided. The soapsuds stank of carbolic, and the stable floor would appear clean only to horses.

He made for the taproom, looking for some ale to accompany his pipe. A figure was slumped in the corner seat by the fire: Jack Douglas. Behind him a gun was propped against the wall. McLevy wondered how the young man had spent the afternoon. He had not seen him at the tinchel.

'Who won the archery contest, Mr Douglas?'

Jack raised his head. 'I don't know.' He lurched to his feet, but he was not as drunk as he had first appeared.

McLevy watched his ale being drawn by Mary, and chatted to her as he drank it. Although darkness was beginning to fall the air was still oppressive, the kind of evening when one was driven alternately indoors and out, vainly seeking coolness.

Mary said, 'There will be thunder. A shame for the bonfire on Ben Correach.'

McLevy saw Jack Douglas rise and lift his coat from the wooden settle beneath the window. He leaned over the sill, his attention caught by something outside.

'What are you doing here?' asked a voice. 'Come back with us, there's a good fellow.'

'Who's us?'

'Clark and myself. The guvnor's invited him to Kilcorrie for the evening.'

'Don't know him.' Jack sat down on the bench with a bleary yawn.

Miles Hatterton walked into the taproom. 'My aunt's solicitor. A tall chap with a beard, going grey.'

'Oh, that fellow. He's still in the sitting-room. I didn't feel conversational.'

Miles dropped his voice. 'Don't sulk, Douglas. I'll keep to what we agreed on. Bachelor quarters tonight.'

There was a growling mutter from Jack.

'I'm in a deuced hurry. We're supposed to show at the peat house before the guvnor opens the ball with Alice.'

Jack finished putting on his coat. 'You're cutting it fine. It's after eight already.'

Miles left the taproom, calling over his shoulder, 'I'm going to find Clark. Ask them to lend us a trap, old man.'

At a quarter past seven Jimmy Dewar slid off the end of a bench in the peat house and thrust his way outside. The speeches were beginning. He'd jink away until the fiddles started up and they broached the whisky.

Meantime, where could he pass the next hour? Daft to pay for drink with all the free liquor ahead. The McIvers owed him something after that stushie about the millstone. Hector and Donald would likely go to the peat house, but Janet would have to put the bairns to bed. If she was alone she'd maybe give him more than a seat by the fire. Jimmy sucked in his cheeks and grinned. She wasn't that old at all. Nothing like ages with Isa. He'd go up by the millstream; fewer folk to spy him t han on the public road. He headed towards the McIvers' cottage.

As he followed the stream uphill the leaf mould began to clog his boots, but the thought of Janet McIver pulled him on. Near the top he began to plod across the wood, keeping the peat road to his right. The grey light was even dimmer among the trees.

After a while, the wood thinned and he could make out the McIvers' cottage. The reek of peat was strong in his nostrils. There was someone moving about the garden.

At the same moment Jimmy heard voices near him. He stopped, wondering whether he'd been seen. A sudden shot made him duck. Guns had been going off ever since he left the peat house, but not so loud. There was a flicker of movement further up the hill and now a dragging, rustling sound that was definitely coming closer. It stopped, and was followed by gasps of deep breathing.

Jimmy peered from behind a tree, watching in fascinated horror. The gloaming must be playing tricks on his eyes. But he *was* seeing right. It put him in mind of warlocks and witches and the loathsome things they got up to in the old days.

Then he panicked. What if he'd been noticed on his way up the burn and someone knew he'd been a witness to *that*? He held his breath to suffocation, staring at the bright green moss beneath his boots.

When the crackling and rustling had ceased he inched his head round the bole of the tree. Nothing moving. No one there.

His knees cracked as he uncurled himself. He ran downhill, tripping a couple of times, snapping off decayed saplings as he clutched to prevent a fall. He ran on despite the thumping in his lungs, not stopping until he was back in the yard of Corrie Castle.

They were carrying the tables out of the peat house, and he could hear fiddles being tuned inside. Folk were standing around waiting for the dances to begin.

Jimmy forced himself to slow down. He strolled through the crowd towards the drive. There he met a man trundling a barrow of whisky jars. He asked jokingly why was Jimmy running away.

When he reached the Dunfillan Arms he stopped to pick up his clothes and tool-bag. Thank God the policeman wasn't there. It'd be mirk dark before he reached home, and his feet would be in blisters. To hell with that, provided he was eight miles out of Kilcorrie when the news got round.

Chapter Fourteen

McLevy could hear the music and shouting inside the peat house as soon as he set out along the village street. There were beacons flaming on four of the hilltops, and small bonfires illuminated the drive of Corrie Castle. A larger one blazed in its central courtyard. The ruined walls had been decorated with coloured lamps, turning the whole frontage into a theatrical façade.

The peat house was on the other side of the courtyard. It was of considerable size, having once held the dried turves for the castle as well as the home farm.

McLevy reached it at the same time as a party of runners in Highland dress who were escorting the Enderby victoria. They flung their torches into the bonfire, and their clapping and cheering brought the dancers outside.

There were only three people in the carriage. Miles helped down his wife and mother-in-law, and the crowd fell back into two lines as he took them inside on his arms. On the threshold they paused to glance round.

'He isn't here, Mama,' said Alice.

Mrs Enderby gave her fan an exasperated flick. 'Why didn't you bring him back with you, Miles?'

'I thought he'd be waiting for us here, Mater. He must have left after all.'

McLevy followed the Kilcorrie party into the peat house. They went to sit on chairs at the far end of the room and watched the dancing as the fiddlers struck up again. The floor began to vibrate under the thud of feet, setting the oil lamps swinging. A smoky haze already blurred the air below the rafters.

After ten minutes of frenetic bowing, the fiddlers laid aside their instruments and clustered round a whisky jar, holding out their horn cups. Mrs Enderby crossed over to them, spoke a few words, and beckoned Miles to her side. McLevy saw the glint of silver being handed over. A piper took over from the fiddlers. Alice walked across the floor.

'Have you seen my father, Mr McLevy? He drove down to the tenants' dinner.'

'I have been here only a few minutes, Mrs Hatterton.'

Miles came up to them and replaced Alice's hand on his arm. 'Those catgut fellows think he walked home after the dinner.'

'That is impossible, Miles! We would have met him on the road. It was half past eight when we drove from the house.' She smiled at McLevy. 'At least we have our own detective officer to investigate his disappearance.'

They left the peat house to return to Kilcorrie.

As the guests drove up the avenue the blaze of light from the dining-room threw the rest of the house into darkness. It had been cleared for dancing and the refectory table now stood in the hall, laid for supper. The ball opened at ten o'clock. There was still no sign of Henry Enderby.

At the end of the first waltz music continued to be played, but slowly. After several minutes leaping bursts of colour outside tore open the darkness; rockets snapped and whistled, and the rose-beds appeared and vanished in glittering cascades of fire.

The dancers surged to the windows to watch. When the display of fireworks was over they streamed into the hall and fell on the first service of refreshments.

A moment after a quarter to eleven, at the end of a

cotillion, the music ceased altogether. A dozen servants entered the ballroom and snuffed out the wax lights. Unlatching the windows, they invited the guests to step on to the terrace. The ladies were offered their wraps.

Miles took Alice's hand. 'This is another surprise from your pater.'

He helped her step over the sill. The balustrade was outlined against a semi-circle of torches stretching the full length of the terrace.

Alice ran forward with a cry of delight, and the men below raised a cheer. As they swayed their torches towards her, the smoky orange light flickered over a pile of deer carcases on the flower-beds. Alice recoiled.

Miles said, 'They're honouring the stags. The gillies are going to dance for you.'

The torches closed in around the deer, leaving enough space for a piper and the dancers, who began their reel by tossing cupfuls of whisky over the antlers. Whirling vigorously, the gillies twined through the figures with increasingly raucous shouts.

Alice was watching the tap of the piper's foot. Her breathing quickened as she leaned against Miles.

'I wish we might be on our own.'

'Only fellows are allowed to say spoony things like that.'

'Can't I say it too now that we're married?'

'My wife has to do what I tell her, Lissie.'

Alice twisted round to face him. 'Don't call me Lissie!'

'That's still Jack's privilege, is it?' He laughed as she tried to break through the tightened circle of his arms.

Alice became still. 'I am not yet *properly* your wife.'

Miles let her pull away from him. She walked off.

'Where are you going?'

'See if you can catch me!' She ran along the back of the crowd lining the balustrade.

Miles stood for a moment before following her. Alice

hurried across the darkened ballroom; when she reached the hall she ran to the far end of the long refreshment table and stopped. Miles chased her round the table, while the servants clapped and laughed.

Several times Alice almost let Miles catch her, but broke away again, her laughter becoming more and more disordered.

At last she darted out of the hall towards the back door. Apart from a few oil lamps the passage was in deep shadow.

She hid herself in the gun room behind a projecting cupboard. She was breathing unevenly, but was not out of breath; her fingers were clasping and unclasping as she waited for Miles to find her. She heard his footsteps pound along the corridor. There was the sound of the back door being opened.

'Alice! Where are you?'

His voice sounded stern, making her smile in the semi-darkness. She waited until he had entered the house again, and peeped from the gun room doorway to make sure he was on his way back to the hall.

When he was halfway along the corridor she slipped out through the back door and shouted, 'Miles, catch me!'

She tiptoed across the yard, feeling the cobbles through her thin ball slippers. Outside the deer larder she hesitated. The ponies had heard her and were shifting in their stalls. There was a flash of lightning across the sky. Her forehead was aching from the close air.

Miles had returned to the doorway, but this time he was carrying one of the oil lamps. Alice called out to attract his attention.

'I'm here, Miles.' She tried to make her voice sound ghostly and had to repress the laughter with a hand across her mouth.

'Come inside again, you silly girl.' He sounded even sterner.

Alice hummed his favourite music-hall song, with her arms stretched across the larder doorway. She wondered if the sound would rouse the dogs in their kennels. She was afraid of the staghounds. She went on humming, but began to lose her accurate pitch.

The advancing lantern was disconnected from the blur of her husband's face; Miles's evening clothes had disappeared against the other blackness.

Alice stepped back against the larder door, which creaked open behind her. She kept her eyes on the swinging point of light; its slow approach stirred up a pleasurable thrill of fear.

She stopped humming and said in a normal voice, 'Miles, here I am.'

He stood and looked at her, the lantern now throwing a clear light on his hands and face. He made an unexpected lunge. Alice turned round and threw herself into the deer larder at the same moment as the sky broke open with a cannonade of thunder.

It was as if she had run into a gigantic spider's web; but she realised almost at once that her face was buried in folds of cloth. They resisted stiffly for a moment before swinging backwards.

Alice stumbled and fell against the stone table. Its hard edge knocked away her breath.

She tried to push herself upright but her hands were sliding through some sticky liquid. She stood up, and the cloth fell over her head again, this time with the rancid odour of ammonia. She fought her way out as Miles and his lantern flooded the place with light.

The layers of crinoline were swaying to and fro. Two feet dangled below them. Alice looked up: above the bell of the skirt a woman's torso was swinging from an iron rail that was clamped to the ceiling.

The rail carried a dozen butcher's hooks. One of them had been driven through the woman's throat and into the under-jaw. The point emerged between her teeth and was glinting in the lantern light.

The woman's clothes were smeared with a dark wetness that had also dripped on to the table, where it lay in a half-coagulated pool. Alice looked down at her own gown and held out her sticky hands to the lantern light. Blood. Outside the rain began to fall with the gushing sound of a waterfall.

Before she began to scream she took another look at the perforated head, and recognised Mrs Vesey.

Chapter Fifteen

McLevy hadn't enjoyed himself so much for years, yet soon after eleven he left the peat house. Jeanie Brash would need a walk before they turned in. He drank off a final dram, waved to his last partner, and stumbled home through the rain pulling a sack round his head and shoulders.

At first he interpreted the sound as another clatter of thunder from the storm which had gathered and broken again before he fell asleep. The sound changed into a steady knocking at his door.

'Rise up, Mr McLevy! You're wanted up at the big house!'

Mrs Gregory rushed in and set down the candle that had illuminated her face in the doorway. That summons was too familiar to be ignored. He was fully dressed in five minutes. The landlady threw her late husband's overcoat on his shoulders as he hurried to the front door.

'The lad can tell you more nor me.'

There was a gig waiting outside; its side-lamps flared through the spitting drops of rain. McLevy scrambled beside the driver, a young man in the Enderby livery.

'It's Mr McLaren sent me, sir, no the laird.'

There had been an accident. The doctor hadn't said what it was. Only that he must bring back Mr McLevy.

The journey was made without further conversation because the groom had to keep his attention on the road. As the pony was trotting up the drive, McLevy saw that the dancers were still circling behind the lighted windows. Whatever had happened, they hadn't stopped the ball.

The yard at the back of the house was dark except for a wedge of light from the deer larder. Against its brightness was silhouetted a man in a mackintosh cape. He stepped forward as the gig drew up.

'Well done, Williams. You know your next errand. As quick as you can, but don't flog the pony to death.'

The driver turned the gig round and drove out of the yard. The man in the cape shook McLevy's hand.

'I am John Maxwell, procurator-fiscal for central Perthshire.' He described what had happened. 'Come inside. She's not a pretty sight.'

Dr Sandy was bending over the stone table. He was wearing a housemaid's kitchen apron and had rolled up his shirt sleeves.

McLevy went to look at the body stretched out on the table. Above the throat the features were contorted into a loose-tongued grin. The top of her gown was stiff with dried blood.

Dr Sandy said angrily, 'I couldn't leave her gaffed on that hook until Cairns arrived.'

He and his sister had been among the first to return indoors after the gillies' dance. Flora had wanted to be taken into supper, he said. They were standing by the central table with a few other guests when Miles Hatterton had called down to him from the gallery. He took Dr Sandy into Alice's bedroom. There Mrs Enderby was trying to restrain her daughter, who was throwing herself about the bed, screaming into her pillow.

'I always carry my bag with me. I gave her a calming dose. Miles said she hadn't stopped since she saw the body.'

Maxwell added, 'Like a sensible chap he carried her upstairs and sent for Mrs Enderby.'

McLevy had been studying the ghastly jaw. 'Have you told Mr Enderby?'

There was a silence. Maxwell cleared his throat. 'We can't find him. We've been all over the house. Williams is driving to Dunfillan for Dr Cairns. He'll also wake up the stationmaster and have a telegraph sent to Perth. Dr Cairns will bring the Dunfillan sergeant back with him.'

'The sheriff's officers should be here by the first morning train,' said Dr Sandy.

McLevy described the scene he had witnessed between Abby Vesey and Mr Enderby. There was another silence.

Maxwell said, 'The ball lasts until dawn. Enderby may be back by breakfast time.'

McLevy saw they had already discussed the implications of their host's absence.

'What if Mr Enderby isn't back for breakfast, sir?'

'We can't detain half the county while we're looking for him. I shall ask for the guest list. The chief constable must be told, of course. He's shooting in Ross-shire.'

'Archie Veitch is here,' said Dr Sandy.

'I know he's the sheriff-substitute, but –' Mr Maxwell looked unhappy.

'You should tell him right away while McLevy takes a look round the larder.'

When they were alone the doctor said, 'Awkward for Maxwell if Enderby's done it. As well as being the local fiscal his firm manages the Kilcorrie estates.'

McLevy asked, 'When do you suppose Mrs Vesey was killed?'

'*Rigor mortis* is almost complete, so it could have happened some time this afternoon. But the surroundings make that only a guess.'

McLevy nodded. The larder faced north and was lined with stone slabs. There were water troughs set against the walls, both to wash the deer joints and to keep down the temperature. Even with the onset of darkness the larder was colder than the outside air.

'Was she killed by – that?' He gestured at the dangling hooks.

'No, she was strangled first. The hyoid arch is broken. Cairns will corroborate my findings.'

In size the larder was roughly equivalent to a cattle-byre. The narrow, unglazed windows would not let in much light even in daytime. McLevy lifted the oil lamp from the table and began to search. At the far end he stooped to pick up something which he showed to Dr Sandy.

'Several hairpins have dropped from her hair. There are two on the table. I wouldn't expect to find one at that end unless Mrs Vesey walked in here alive.'

John Maxwell returned. 'I've spoken to Veitch. He agrees we should say nothing until morning. That fellow from the *Perthshire Advertiser* is scribbling his report of the ball. I think he'll be off by six. We'll question the guests after he's left.'

'The *Advertiser* doesn't come out until next Thursday.'

'Yes, Balinmore; but there's the *Reporter* on Saturday and all the national journals. I'll have another word with Hatterton.'

'And I'll continue my examination,' said Dr Sandy.

McLevy walked behind the fiscal into the hall, where the guests were consuming a second supper. The fiscal introduced McLevy to the bridegroom.

Miles said, 'I've told everyone that Alice has retired with a headache.' Maxwell nodded approval. Miles's tone changed. 'What a terrible business! We were larking round the table and then we went out to the yard. I let Alice run into *that*!'

The fiscal wrung his arm. 'Don't blame yourself, Miles. McLevy, please don't go questioning anyone else. We don't want those newspaper fellows on our heels.' He walked away.

This was McLevy's first encounter with Jack's fortunate rival. He saw a massively handsome man whose stolidity appeared unruffled by the violent event, except for the way his eyes flinched on meeting McLevy's.

'I'd like to get my hands on the blackguard who did it!' he burst out. 'My wife was devoted to Abby.'

McLevy said, 'Our best hope is to find Mr Enderby. When was the last time you saw him, sir?'

Miles glanced round the crowded hall. 'Let's go up to the gallery.'

Hanging over the rail he went on, 'Enderby and I were both late setting out for the tinchel. I'd received a letter which I went to discuss with my wife. Enderby was waiting for me at the back of the house. The others had left.'

'Did you walk to the deer drive with him?'

'No, he said he'd meet me in the beech clearing, but he'd gone by the time I arrived – that was three o'clock. Must have been in a hurry to get to the tinchel.'

'What did you do between speaking to Mr Enderby and walking to the clearing?'

'I went up to my room to answer Clark's letter. On the way I called in at the kitchen to arrange for someone to carry my reply to the village. Upstairs I spent about ten minutes having a look for my seal. Then I hurried after Enderby. Didn't see him until I reached the dykes.'

The young man pulled at his fair moustache, one side after the other, and then smoothed it with his forefinger.

'Have to admit I was as frightened as Alice. The larder was empty the last time I saw it.'

'When was that, sir?'

'I was poking around before luncheon on Wednesday. Curious about the place, you see. Went back on Thursday morning to hunt for the seal – remembered my watch chain catching on a nail in the wall. No luck.' He frowned.

McLevy sighed at the meandering nature of Captain Hatterton's recollections. 'This letter you wrote, sir. What time did you hand it to the servant?'

'I was to meet Clark after the tinchel anyway, so I didn't finish it. Gave up after I couldn't find my seal.'

'Did you walk back with Mr Enderby after the deer drive?'

'No. I called off the staghounds, and then I watched the people gut the deer. I came home with the ponies.'

'Did you speak to him after you had both returned to Kilcorrie?'

'Yes, some time between five and six, I suppose.'

'I'm told Mr Enderby attended the tenants' dinner. You didn't see him when you came down to bathe in the stables?'

Miles looked uncomfortable. 'I was jolly careful not to. The guvnor wanted the whole family to attend the dinner, but Mrs E wasn't keen.'

'You mean there was a disagreement about it?'

'Well, some hot words at breakfast. They agreed on a short visit afterwards. Mama-in-law gave me a wigging when I got back to the house with Clark. She was waiting in the carriage to set out for the peat house. She was furious the guvnor wasn't with us.'

McLevy looked over the gallery rail. John Maxwell was facing Mrs Enderby. She was tapping her fan against her palm, and he was eating syllabub. They might have been holding an ordinary conversation; but the hostess had turned her back on the hall.

'Surely there was some anxiety about Mr Enderby's disappearance, even by eight o'clock?'

Miles said apologetically, 'It sounds damn silly, McLevy, but we kept thinking we'd missed him. Mrs E asked Balinmore to help her receive the guests. Later she told Alice a downright fib, that the guvnor had taken some fellows to the library for a smoke.'

'When was that?'

'Before we went out for the gillies' dance, and *that* was not long before eleven.'

'By then Mrs Enderby would be seriously alarmed?'

Miles nodded. 'So was I, but what could we do?'

After taking Alice to her bedroom and fetching her mother and Dr Sandy, Miles had searched for Mr Enderby.

'That was soon after half past eleven. McLaren asked me to have another look round the house with Maxwell and said he'd send for you.'

'Did you find anything to suggest that Mr Enderby returned to the house after the tenants' dinner?'

'Not a trace, old chap. He must have sortied in and out.'

McLevy saw comprehension awaken in the bridegroom's mind. Miles leaned against the gallery banisters and blew a gasp of surprise at the ceiling. 'By Jove! I wondered about all those questions. Poor old Abby!'

'We have no explanation at present,' said McLevy guardedly.

'What shall you do next?'

'I'll try to discover what Mrs Vesey was doing during the afternoon. When it's light we shall look for Mr Enderby, if he hasn't returned by then.'

Captain Hatterton's face lit up. 'I'll get up a search party. Don't have to wait till dawn.'

The detective made his face carefully blank. 'That's handsome of you, sir, but you will wish to remain beside Mrs Hatterton.'

'The medico won't let me near her. She's sleeping like – I beg your pardon.'

Miles was so disconcerted that McLevy felt sorry for him.

'Slip of the tongue, sir. Anyone could have said it.'

He made his way downstairs. Apart from the missing Dundreary whiskers Miles Hatterton was the very model of a 'heavy swell' as satirised by *Punch*. Yet McLevy was not convinced that he was totally baffled by his father-in-law's disappearance. He had been very reticent when asked about the quarrel between Mr and Mrs Enderby.

Chapter Sixteen

The servants were clearing the remains of the supper, but a side buffet had been set out on three smaller tables ranged along the wall. McLevy was famished. He heaped a plate with mixed remnants and seated himself in a corner of the hall.

As he ate he decided to ask the fiscal for permission to search Mrs Vesey's room, but when he put down the empty plate he found that Mr Maxwell had returned to the ballroom. The fiscal was pulling on his gloves, on the point of leading his partner into a waltz.

He said in a carefully lowered voice, 'Nothing of interest in there, McLevy. I've already had a thorough search.'

McLevy walked back to the hall, knotting his ungloved hands in frustration. His mind kept returning to the scene between Abby Vesey and Mr Enderby. Had her message made him desperate enough to silence her? If anyone could find a plausible excuse to lure Abby Vesey into the larder, it would be Mr Enderby.

McLevy walked up and down the hall beneath the sporting trophies, trying to pace off his annoyance with the fiscal as he inspected the cases of glassy-eyed fish and wild-cats. It seemed odd that such a keen stalker had not hung up any antlers.

While he was reading the metal labels Flora McLaren glided up behind him. He put the point to her.

'You would find plenty of antlers in the library, I am told. Mr Enderby prefers ladies not to enter it.'

McLevy thought he saw a prevaricating glint in Miss McLaren's eyes; but before he could pursue it Dr Sandy spoke behind them.

'Flora, would you please take Mrs Enderby's place beside Alice? She wishes to shorten the programme of dances.'

'How is Mrs Hatterton?' McLevy asked as Flora went upstairs.

'I'm keeping her husband away from her.' Dr Sandy chuckled unkindly. 'Hatterton'll have to wait for his kisses.' He looked at his watch. 'Two o'clock! Isobel will have locked the outer door.' His jaws clenched on a yawn.

Weariness was also beginning to creep up on McLevy, but he had thought of a way to circumvent John Maxwell.

He said, 'I'll see if the folk in the kitchen remember how Mrs Vesey spent the afternoon.' Luck or wit would suggest some way to avoid rousing their suspicions.

'And I must go back to the larder. Cairns and the sergeant will soon be here.'

The kitchen was emptier and less busy than McLevy had expected. The servants were sitting round the long deal table nibbling at the leftovers. He discovered that most of them had been hired from a Perth agency for the season, and a dozen more taken on for the wedding celebrations. Only a few of their own staff had accompanied the Enderbys from London.

A young footman recognised McLevy's description.

'Yon English body, who was aye getting in our road?'

'She left the kitchen at about half-past two. Can you remember what was happening then?'

The young man shook his head. 'Only that the captain put his head in and said he'd send for someone to take a letter to the village.'

McLevy asked for the housekeeper, and was told that Mrs Frazer had retired to the cook's sitting-room. He tapped at the door and found both women inside. Might he have a word?

Mrs Frazer asked if he'd come about Mrs Maxwell's brooch. She'd advise him not to get into a creel about *that*. Last month the fiscal's lady complained about a diamond breast-pin that later turned up in the slop-water.

McLevy humoured her mistake and managed to guide the conversation to Abby Vesey. The two women confirmed that she had been an irritant in the overworked kitchen. There was personal dislike as well; Mrs Frazer presided at Kilcorrie all year round and Mrs Vesey had been given what the housekeeper called her 'work room', which had its own row of bells. Mrs Frazer deeply resented being summoned through the public system in the kitchen.

Had Mrs Vesey made a particular friend of any of the staff?

The cook answered, 'There's yon red-headed lass, Mairi Hamilton. Yesterday Mistress Vesey and Mairi went upstairs with a tray of tea.'

'Aye, but she's away like the most of them,' said Mrs Frazer.

'They bespoke a cart to catch the early train.'

The cook suggested, 'Peggy would ken where to find Mairi Hamilton.' They both seemed to think that she was suspected of taking the brooch.

McLevy returned to the kitchen; remembering Dr Sandy's repressed yawn, he yawned himself. He asked for Peggy, whom he persuaded to make up his cure for drowsiness. While this was brewing he asked why she hadn't gone back to Perth with the others.

Peggy went into an involved account of her mother having broken a wrist and being laid off work at the umbrella-gingham mill. She herself had asked to stay on another week for the sake of the extra wages.

'Will your mother not be wondering where you are?'

'Mairi'll cry in and tell her.'

'I hear your friend Mairi got in with Mrs Vesey.'

'Oh, her!' There was a jealous curl to Peggy's lip. 'She blethered on about getting Mairi a place in London, but it was all flim-flam. Mairi has to get back to her bairns.'

'Where does Mairi stay, Peggy?'

'We're neighbours in the Kirkgate. My mother and my wee sister looked after the bairns while Mairi was here.'

The girl filled the coffee pot and set it on a wooden tray with three cups. 'There you are, sir. Shall I carry it for you?'

'Thank you, but I'll see to that myself. What were you and Mairi doing about half-past two yesterday?'

'Packing up jellies frae the wedding. We had to send them to the peat house.'

McLevy took this as a generic description of the marquee refreshments. 'Was Mrs Vesey in the kitchen at the time?'

Peggy frowned. 'I'm no sure. She was in and out all forenoon. Later on she went to speak to the laird, and came back looking like she'd seen a bogle. She telt us Mr Enderby said she was to drink some tea in her room.'

'How long did it take to brew that?'

'I'd just made a pot for Mrs Frazer, and Mairi lifted it right under my nose. "You just take this, Abby," she said. Then the two of them went up the stair with it.'

McLevy asked what Mrs Vesey had been talking about before she went to speak to Mr Enderby.

'I didna pay heed. I was buckling into my work,' said Peggy self-righteously.

'Please try to remember.'

'Something about it no being Christian to be married outside a kirk. We were speaking about Scotch marriage – well, Mairi was,' amended Peggy hastily. 'Then Mrs Vesey went all pale and she fleed out like a scalded cat.'

'Did Mairi say anything when she returned from Mrs Vesey's room?'

'Me and Mairi's cast out since yon pot of tea. We're no speaking. I'll give her a hard time when I see her in Perth.'

McLevy took his tray to the yard behind the house. It was no longer raining, but the cobbles were still wet and slippery. He breathed in the chilly freshness, and his miasma of fatigue began to lift. The sun would not rise for another hour and a half, but a few birds were chirping and the sky had begun to lighten over the black mass of woods behind Kilcorrie.

The sergeant from Dunfillan was now standing guard by the larder door. Behind him McLevy saw Dr Sandy and his colleague rinsing their hands in a stone tub of water. The body was covered with a cloth.

The two doctors came out of the larder as McLevy set down his tray on a mounting block.

Dr Sandy rubbed his hands. 'Just what I need.' He lifted his cup with a smile, but spat out the first mouthful, his lips writhing as if he had bitten a lemon. 'What hell's broth is this, McLevy?'

'Coffee brewed in vinegar. It never fails to keep me awake.'

As they returned their cups to the tray, Flora McLaren burst into the yard. She ran over to clutch her brother's arm.

'Sandy, please come indoors! Alice is in a dreadful state. She has wakened from a nightmare.'

'Give her another small dose. It won't harm her.'

Flora led her brother to one side. McLevy saw dismay spread over the doctor's face. He returned to the two men.

'Cairns, I'd be obliged if you would finish in there. I'll see you later about the report for the fiscal.'

He hurried after his sister. In the doorway he turned round and looked at McLevy. The detective walked over.

'What is the matter, Balinmore?'

'Alice told Flora that she has killed her father.'

Chapter Seventeen

McLevy was sitting in a corner of the staircase gallery; his nostrils were filled with the steamy fragrance of tea. A few minutes only, he had promised himself as he sank into the crimson-fringed armchair.

'What is the time, Miss McLaren?'

'It wants a few minutes to six o'clock. I have brought you this.'

His remedy had failed him. He had slept for nearly two hours while Mrs Enderby, Flora and Dr Sandy were closeted with Alice. They had taken Mr Maxwell with them.

There was a change in his surroundings, and it was not the early morning light streaming through the clerestory windows of the hall.

Flora said, 'You will notice that the music has ceased.'

That was it. When he had fallen asleep the guests were still dancing. The last sound he remembered was of violins playing a schottische. Now there was silence except for a murmur of voices.

Flora said, 'They have found Mr Enderby.'

McLevy rose to his feet. 'Why did you not awaken me, Miss McLaren?'

'How could I do so, you foolish man, when I did not know where you were? Mr Enderby is dead. My brother is examining his injuries with Mr Maxwell. Dr Cairns returned to Dunfillan before he was discovered. There has been an accident. He was crushed by a millstone.'

She described how four men had found the body in the woods and carried it to Kilcorrie on an improvised bier of larch branches. It had been taken up the service stairs to Mr Enderby's dressing-room.

'When did this happen?'

'They brought him home fifteen minutes ago. Young Donald McIver ran ahead with the news.'

The voices in the hall were speaking with hushed intensity. McLevy walked to the top of the stairs and saw small groups of guests with their heads drawn together. Half a dozen servants were handing out armfuls of outdoor clothing.

He watched as most of the guests departed. They made no farewells. The house became so quiet that the loudest noise was the crunch of wheels on gravel outside the front door.

McLevy turned back to Flora. 'A *millstone*, you said?'

'Yes, a new one was cut from a rock in the woods behind Corrie Castle. It seems that the men went to roll it down to the mill early this morning and it ran away. When they overtook it they found Mr Enderby lying beneath.'

'Are the men still here?'

'Mr Maxwell has spoken to them, but he allowed them to go away. He said he would take their formal statements at the Dunfillan Arms. He will have to wait for the sheriff's officers.'

'Well?' challenged McLevy, sipping the tea. 'What does this have to do with Mrs Hatterton?' He had felt nettled by his exclusion.

Flora held his gaze over the rim of the cup. 'Please excuse me, Mr McLevy. I must return to Mrs Enderby... Oh, was there anything significant in Mrs Vesey's room?'

'How did you know?' He was vexed that she had seen him.

'You were coming out of the door when I went to fetch some negus for Mrs Hatterton. I too wondered whether some clue might lie inside that room.'

'There was nothing to throw light on Mrs Vesey's murder.'

He had noticed one detail which might explain how Abby had been persuaded to leave her room, but he was not going to discuss that with Miss McLaren. It was after his search that he had fallen asleep.

Other servants were now carrying breakfast dishes to the sideboard, but the few people left in the hall seemed disinclined to eat. McLevy walked down to the hall, rubbing at the bristle on his cheeks. It was a grey, watery morning. The smell of burnt-out candle wax blended with the odours of bacon, kidneys and eggs. He must have slept deeply; the large refectory table had vanished, presumably taken back to the ballroom.

He lifted the silver covers on the sideboard and after helping himself to a navvy's plateful went to sit at one of the tables set against the wall.

The remaining guests frowned their disapproval; but indignation soon gave way to hunger and within a few moments most of them were eating beside him, although with a sombre air.

'What a ghastly accident,' muttered a white-haired man to McLevy's left. 'Those fools, letting the stone run away!'

McLevy nodded wearily. He had spent the evening dancing with energetic young women, and his interrupted sleep had not refreshed him.

Common sense rejected the mode of Mr Enderby's death. It was almost as incredible that he should have died at all. Now it would be ten times harder to find out whether he had murdered Mrs Vesey.

McLevy thought about Alice Enderby's claim that she had killed her father. It could only be a nightmare, but what a strange coincidence after her behaviour on the drive to the Falls of Tummel.

Before he had finished eating Flora McLaren came to sit beside him. Her plate was nearly as well heaped as his own. McLevy put down his knife and fork.

'Is Mr Maxwell free to see me?'

'He left for the village a few moments ago with Captain Hatterton. They have taken some of the servants to search the woods. We must be patient until Sandy has finished his examination.'

McLevy stood up. He had no intention of being patient. He excused himself and returned to the kitchen. A hush fell on the servants as he entered; ten pairs of eyes lifted from their breakfast plates.

He asked for Mrs Frazer; as if summoned she came out of the cook's private room. McLevy drew her aside.

'Did anyone besides Mr Maxwell speak to the men who brought home Mr Enderby's body?'

'Rob Brodie, the keeper, sir. Donald ran to him first with the news. He's away with the captain and Mr Maxwell, but he'll only walk the length of the policies with them.'

She took McLevy into the back courtyard and pointed at a track heading in the direction of the village. It was a continuation of the path along which the shooting party had set out for Bealach nan Bo.

'That's him now on the peat road.'

McLevy advanced to meet the man limping towards the house. He was dressed in ginger-coloured tweeds and leaning on a stick. His face was covered by a grizzled mass of beard and whiskers.

'Mr Brodie?'

'Aye. Who might you be?' What could be seen of the keeper's features was weathered into gaunt creases.

'James McLevy, an Edinburgh police officer. I am asking some questions on behalf of Mr Maxwell. Would you please repeat what Donald McIver told you about the accident with the millstone?'

'Aye, what he *told* me.'

McLevy gestured at a fallen trunk and offered his tobacco pouch. When they were seated, Rob Brodie eased out his left leg.

He said the dancing and drinking had continued in the peat house until dawn. Hector McIver and three other men had left at four o'clock to fetch the millstone.

'No that I was there that long myself,' said Brodie dourly.

They had cut down a larch sapling to push through the open eye of the stone and trundle it along the peat road. The route they took dropped down the hill enclosing the north side of the Pass of Crannich.

Brodie waved at some beeches at the edge of the wood. 'Over yonder, but you canna see the path for the trees. It was slippy with the rain, they said. Coming down the brae the stone just wheeched out of their hands.'

'Why did they take such a circuitous route? Would it not be simpler to roll the stone straight down the hill?'

The mill stood beside a burn that ran under the glen road into the Crannich. McLevy had seen it among the buildings clustered around the ruined walls of Corrie Castle.

'The ground's far ower soft. They meant to get it out by the gate on the glen road. They had a pony waiting there. I trust *that* part of their story.'

'You think they're lying?'

The reply was ambiguous. 'Donald was on his way here to hang the venison. He passed the others, and then he heard the stone running through the trees. It was him found the laird.'

'What do you think happened, Mr Brodie?'

The keeper gave McLevy a sideways glance. 'It's weel kent where the laird walks before his breakfast. Maybe Hector McIver set the stone loose.'

'How large is it?'

'About three foot span.'

'So the captain has gone to spy out whether Mr Enderby was visible from the point where the stone broke loose?'

'You're the devil himself, Mr McLevy!'

The detective smiled wryly. It was not a new accusation, but the first time it had been intended as a compliment.

'You are making a grave charge. Why should Hector McIver try to kill Mr Enderby?'

'He's to lose the croft in May. The laird wants to take it back into the estate.'

'That's nine months away.'

'Aye, but yesterday...' He paused.

'Go on.'

'There's been a row about the chap mending the dykes. Hector telt Jimmy Dewar to cut a stone for the Corrie mill. The old one split in March. We didna find that out till the Saturday. The laird was raging like a bull, because Jimmy should have been mending the dykes. He sent me to speak to Donald McIver – I'd telt him to let Jimmy ken what there was to do.'

McLevy remembered the quarrel between the two brothers in the Dunfillan Arms. 'Why is Hector so anxious to fit up the mill?'

'The crofters thresh and grind right through the winter, just when they need the meal. But Hector wants his all done at once. He means to sell it to help pay for his flitting in May.'

'Had the mason finished the new stone?'

'Aye, but the laird sent word it was no to be fitted to the mill. You mind when the shooting party set out to the tinchel? I dropped off to fetch my pony, and I went inby the house for a minute. When I came out there was Hector waiting on me.'

The Brodies occupied what had once been the head gardener's cottage, which was situated near Kilcorrie House and the peat road running along the edge of the woods. The keeper had found Hector doubled over by the porch, apparently in agonising pain.

'He was retching like a dog. I kent it was just his black temper over the millstone. I said the laird was pulling down the mill in October and he'd have to take his turn at Inverconan with the rest.'

'Is it far to the Inverconan mill?'

'A mile, just.'

'Did Hector threaten Mr Enderby?'

'No exactly. I telt him he'd never get his meal ground by November and he asked what I meant.' The keeper hesitated again.

'What did you mean, Mr Brodie?'

'The laird was that angry he said he'd put the McIvers out this November, and no wait on till May. He'd just get by Miss Alice's wedding, he telt me, and then send them warning.'

'In heaven's name, why did you pass this on to Hector McIver?'

'I ken it was daft, but I was in a fair rage myself, Mr McLevy. Hector swore at me and ran off through the park.'

'Where did he go?'

'Along this track. It runs behind the big house right on to the village. I saw Hector cross with the laird, but they didna speak. He was up at Kilcorrie at half past eight the same night, asking to see Mr Enderby. He's no right in the head, Mr McLevy.'

Chapter Eighteen

When McLevy returned to the hall he noticed Flora McLaren seated beside her brother, who was attacking his breakfast with excited gestures. The McLarens were in the middle of an argument.

This ceased when he walked up to them. Dr Sandy waved his hand at a pot of coffee. 'Help yourself, McLevy. No vinegar, I promise!'

'Thank you, but I shall return to the village.'

'For what purpose?'

'To enquire why Mr Enderby went to the wood this morning. Captain Hatterton's search party may overlook some traces.'

McLevy's weariness was making him irritable. 'Those men should not have separated the body from the millstone!'

'Enderby didn't walk in the wood this morning. I doubt he walked at all after seven or eight o'clock last night.'

McLevy's surprise did not prevent him from noting that Flora did not share it.

Dr Sandy went on, 'It was a freakish accident that the stone rolled across his body. Enderby was shot... There, Flora, I've told him.' He stood up. 'Come with me, McLevy.'

When Miss McLaren tried to follow them her brother said, 'No, Flora, but not for the propriety of your sex. This is police business.'

Mr Enderby's corpse lay on the bed under a sheet, which Dr Sandy pulled down to waist level. The arms and shrouded bulk of his legs were twisted slightly askew of the rest of his body. There was a jagged, blood-encrusted wound in his chest; it lay in a plate-sized patch of skin surrounded by a pelt of dark hair.

'I had to shave that off. His shirt was glued to his skin. The clothes were sodden with rain, of course. Hector's millstone ran over his abdomen and legs, but I'll not show you that.'

'He was shot from the front?' McLevy's eyes avoided the glaring face.

'The gun was fired from behind. Look.'

Dr Sandy put his hand under the corpse's shoulder and turned it over. It had stiffened into a bow shape. There was another wound at the back of the neck, almost as jagged as the first. The scorched bruising around it was tattooed with particles of gunpowder.

'Just like my scalp, eh? If the stone had rolled over his neck I might have missed that.' Dr Sandy pulled away his hand; the corpse rocked for a second or two on its back.

'What caused that guddle in his chest?'

'Bone splinters tearing the skin. The bullet hit the top of the spine or the shoulder-blade – I can't tell which – and ricocheted through his heart.'

'Was it an accident?'

'He was shot by someone standing as close to him as I am to you. I've written a note for the procurator-fiscal. When you return to the village, would you take it to him? We saw that Enderby had been shot, but nothing more before Maxwell went away. Hatterton's looking for the gun.'

McLevy said, 'No one could approach without being heard. Was the shot fired from an ambush?'

'Quite impossible from the nature of the wound.'

'Then the murderer was walking with him.'

'And it happened shortly after the tinchel.' The doctor

picked up a scalpel and tapped it against the foot of the bed, avoiding McLevy's gaze. 'You know what I'm trying not to say.'

'Let us look at other possibilities. Did Mr Enderby have any enemies in Glencrannich?' McLevy wondered if he would name Hector McIver.

'The crofters disliked him for taking in their leases.'

'What about his farm tenants?'

'Oh, he certainly annoyed *them*. He stole their day-workers whenever his guests needed a gillie. He didn't employ assistants for Rob Brodie, apart from young McIver. None of that seems sufficient reason for murder.'

'Maybe Mr Enderby stumbled over a poacher.'

Dr Sandy gave a bark of laughter and pointed at the chest wound. 'Do you know the cost of an Express rifle? Even Enderby's keepers have to make do with his cast-offs. Donald McIver has a muzzle loader that might have been fired at Waterloo.'

'How can you tell the wound was made by an Express?'

'The bullet hit bone, turned itself around, and still came out like a cannon ball. Nothing else would be powerful enough.'

McLevy stood looking down at the body.

Dr Sandy asked diffidently, 'What do you make of it? Both murders, I mean.'

'Abby Vesey was killed soon after speaking to Mr Enderby. She gave him a dangerous piece of information. That does not prove he committed the murder, but I'm inclined to think he did.'

'It looks as if the secret was as dangerous to him as to Mrs Vesey.'

'Surely you remember their conversation?' said McLevy. 'Whatever Mr Enderby heard was personal to him. I think Mrs Vesey didn't realise its significance. To ensure her silence he would have to kill her. That would be his reason for committing the murder – if he did.'

Dr Sandy sat down at the feet of the corpse and groped inside his breast pocket. 'Why are you so damn sharp, McLevy? Give me a lucifer.'

He lit the cigar clumsily. 'When Alice woke up she clutched on to Flora for dear life. She repeated over and over, "I have killed my father." Had you had seen the look on her face...' He let the match burn between his fingers.

'Dr McLaren, be rational. How could she have done it in the time available? Mr Enderby attended the tenants' dinner, thus he must have been killed after seven o'clock. Mrs Hatterton would have spent at least half an hour dressing. I spoke to her myself a few minutes before nine at the peat house, and she was wearing a ball gown.'

Dr Sandy went on as if he had not heard. 'From the earth and leaves on his coat I'd say the body was dragged across the ground.'

'Mr Enderby was not tall, but corpulent enough to be very heavy. She could not have moved the body any distance.'

Dr Sandy drew the sheet back over the corpse. 'I pray someone else fired the bullet.'

There must be a reason for such perversity. 'Are you certain about the time of death?'

'Aye, there's the rub. Rigor mortis isn't an exact science. You can see the stiffening is almost complete. I believe he was shot between seven and eight last night, but I might be wrong by several hours.'

McLevy thought about this. 'If he was murdered after eight o'clock, you are frighting at shadows. After Mrs Hatterton stepped into the carriage to drive to the peat house she could not have been alone for an instant.'

The doctor lifted one of the enamel dishes beside the bed and crushed his cigar into its muddy fluid.

'If he died earlier, the shadows are very substantial. Yet I'm sure Alice knew nothing about Mrs Vesey's death. I had the devil of a job to calm her. I shall have the body moved out of the larder as soon as possible.'

'May you not be misinterpreting Mrs Hatterton? She was stupefied with laudanum.'

Hands clasped behind his back, Dr Sandy began to pace the room in that swaying straddle learned on the quarter-deck.

'McLevy, you cannot believe that Alice had some premonition of her father's death!'

'No, but last Monday Mrs Hatterton persuaded me to describe a murder case. I spoke about a man who killed his friend and dreamt of their fatal quarrel the night before. She was remarkably distressed.'

'Like bairns with a bed-time story. Fee-fi-fo-fum.'

'There was no fee-fi-fo-fum. She remembered something profoundly horrifying. I believe she has a recurring dream which was revived by my story and the sight of Mrs Vesey's body. After her first visit to Kilcorrie in 1860 Mrs Hatterton suffered from nightmares for six months.'

'Did she, by Jove!' Dr Sandy ruminated for a moment. He said, 'That was the year I was called in a few days before they returned to London. Mrs Enderby heard screams outside her bedroom, and she found Alice clinging to the gallery rail. It was about seven in the morning. Alice went into hysterics and locked herself in her room. It took half an hour to persuade her to open the door.'

'Where was Mr Enderby all this while?'

'Walking round the estate, as usual. He returned not long after Mrs Enderby sent the groom to fetch me. He became most agitated when she told him. He was very attached to his daughter.'

'Do you think Mrs Enderby told the whole truth?'

'No, I don't. Alice screamed when I tried her pulse, so I didn't examine her closely. I think it was women's business, and Mrs Enderby was ashamed to admit that she hadn't warned her daughter. She would be the right age for it. There was blood on the sheets, Flora heard later.'

'Did Miss McLaren mention anything else?'

'No. I don't encourage her to discuss my cases. Besides, she has a deal of secrets with Rose Enderby that she'll not pass on.'

'Well,' said McLevy, 'clearly the distress of that time lives on in Mrs Hatterton's dreams.'

Dr Sandy turned to face the detective. 'Let us suppose your theory correct, and Alice repeatedly dreams that she has killed her father. Her mind must be inhabited by demons! Did you know that young Douglas drinks?'

'I have observed it.' McLevy was baffled by the change of subject.

'We were invited to Kilcorrie for dinner on Tuesday. When the ladies left us he got into his cups and let out that Alice is almost as good a marksman as her husband. Douglas used to take her to his rifle club. Hatterton was furious.'

'M'm,' said McLevy.

'Have you heard any comments about Mrs Vesey being absent when Alice dressed for the ball? One of the servants must have helped her.'

'Nobody in the kitchen mentioned that,' conceded McLevy. 'But there was no reason they should.'

'Flora used the dressing-room opening off Alice's bedroom. Alice wasn't in it, and her hot water was untouched on the wash-stand. That was at half past six.'

'Dr McLaren –'

'Patience, McLevy! Flora noticed Captain Hatterton's clothes and other frippery near the bed. His razor case was unlatched. She went to close it, and saw that one of the razors was missing.'

After she had inspected the case, thought McLevy.

'As Flora was leaving the room she met Miles's valet. He'd been ordered to send Captain Hatterton's evening clothes to the Dunfillan Arms. He said Alice wasn't with his master. Flora went to the drawing-room, but Alice was not there either.'

'What time was this?'

'About seven o'clock. Flora saw Alice mounting the stairs a few minutes after the half hour, still in her afternoon dress. Her shoes were covered with earth.'

'What is the point of your sister's observations?' McLevy was becoming ruffled by Miss McLaren's zeal to assist him.

'Mr Enderby's abdomen is considerably mangled. Crushed by the millstone, of course, but as well as that –'

He went as if to lift the sheet from the body, and then threw it down again. 'After death his virile member was cut off.'

Chapter Nineteen

McLevy went to fetch his coat and top hat, very troubled by Dr Sandy's last piece of information. It fitted in with some intuitions of his own. He reminded himself that Hector McIver must not be discounted as a suspect.

On his way to the front door he passed the dining-room. He came to a halt, clicking his fingers behind his back – a habit for which his sister often reproved him.

The huge mahogany table stood in what must be its usual place. The gleam of the floor had been danced away; strewn across it were wilted flowers from the women's hair and corsages. A few instruments had been left on the musicians' dais, which had not yet been removed. A man was sitting beside one of the stands, plucking at a violin.

McLevy took a sudden decision. He walked across the floor.

'Well, Mr Douglas, this is a grim affair. Two murders. May I ask you some questions?'

Jack's fingers left the strings. 'What do you want to know, McLevy?'

Bluntness seemed the best approach. 'I need some general information about the Enderbys and yourself.'

Jack said with a shrug, 'Very well.'

'Are there any other children?'

'None who survived. Alice was brought up with my sisters.'

He was struggling to keep up a pose of indifference.

'May I ask your opinion of Captain Hatterton?'

Jack looked startled, and then his mouth twisted. It was a face made for scowling, McLevy thought with amusement.

'Miles was a roaring boy until Mrs Melton called him to heel. Knocking off policemen's helmets, high jinks in the mess, betting and gambling. That sort of thing.'

'No recommendation in a son-in-law, surely?'

'He's lived soberly since meeting Alice, but that may not last. On Wednesday night he boasted he could vault across the billiard table with a cue balanced in his palm. It became tangled in his watch chain and scraped the baize. He swore like a bargee.' Jack laughed, but without enjoyment.

'Not a serious misdemeanour, Mr Douglas.' The young man was apparently priggish as well as jealous.

Jack frowned. 'Miles Hatterton is a brute. He kept a ferret at school. On one occasion it slipped its muzzle and he couldn't get it out of the rabbit warren.'

'Ferrets sometimes run amok and fall asleep after the kill, I've heard.'

'The rabbits were squealing below, and then all went quiet. Two weeks later Miles found the animal caged in another part of the grounds.'

'So he stole it back.'

'No, he waited to see who was feeding it. Some other fellow had found it making for home, and he'd been running it at the rabbits himself. Miles paid him to hand over the ferret.'

'None of this sounds brutish to me, Mr Douglas.'

'He starved the animal for a week before killing it for disobedience. He said he had no use for a ferret that someone else had run. I heard that story from Alice.'

The cruelty was revolting; but was there anyone who hadn't committed some barbaric act in childhood? The story proved only that Miss Enderby had confided a great deal about her engagement to Jack Douglas.

'Do you know about Mrs Hatterton's nightmares in the winter of 1860?'

A wary look passed across Jack's face, but it was instantly obliterated. 'Alice mentioned them when she was helping me at the blanket depot in Shoreditch.'

'Did she describe her dreams?'

'She said she was being hunted across a moor, and the heather flowers were the colour of blood.'

McLevy walked at a slow pace to the village. He wanted to think over his information before he had another encounter with Mr Maxwell. He must question Rob Brodie again, and his journey to Edinburgh would have to be postponed.

Like Mary Gregory, Mrs Vesey 'clacked too much'. Had she run to her employer with some secret about Alice? Perhaps Mr Enderby first silenced Mrs Vesey and then confronted his daughter, with fatal results. Miles Hatterton or Jack Douglas might have assisted her.

Alternatively, mother and daughter might have plotted the murder together. Mrs Enderby had quarrelled with her husband, and the reality was certain to be more serious than Captain Hatterton had suggested.

Yet wasn't it fanciful to probe the relationship between the Enderby women and the dead man when he had such a likely suspect in Hector McIver?

As he reached the Dunfillan Arms Miles Hatterton was mounting the box of a handsome green gig, which he drove off towards Kilcorrie House. He raised his whip in greeting as he trotted by.

The side door of the inn was locked. McLevy rapped on an adjacent window pane, behind which Mary Gregory's blonde head was bent over the kitchen sink. She mouthed a few words which he could not make out, but the gesture was clear enough. He was to use the front entrance.

Inside, the hall was full of uniformed police officers. One said to him, 'Sorry, sir, there's no one let in until Mr

Maxwell's finished his examination.'

It was twenty to ten by the hall clock. The electric telegraph had stirred up the whole panoply of the law. It was now being directed against Mr Enderby's killer.

The policeman was unaware that there had been a previous murder; he wondered aloud whether the fatal shot had been fired from the gun which Captain Hatterton had found in the woods.

This reminded McLevy of Dr Sandy's note for the fiscal, and he handed it over.

He was allowed through to the kitchen, where Mary and Mrs Gregory were preparing a meal for the official inquisitors. The curiosity of the summer guests had been thwarted; the fiscal and sheriff-substitute had taken over their sitting-room and sent them on a compulsory excursion.

'I was told something about a gun.'

'Oh, yon! It belongs to Mr Maxwell's laddie. D'you want to speak to him?'

Mary exclaimed, 'It's well seen he's more fashed for his gun than for poor Mr Enderby!'

Mrs Gregory dusted off her floury hands. 'Take Mr McLevy to the wee mannie.'

There was some misunderstanding. McLevy followed Mary to the dining-room, where a youth in crumpled evening clothes was kicking at the empty fireplace. He turned round with an impatient look.

'Are you still not finished?'

Trying to quench an instant dislike, McLevy reminded himself of the sorrows of adolescence. If he wanted to poach this minnow he must not be too touchy himself. He remembered seeing the lad among the sportsmen on Thursday afternoon.

'Mr Maxwell? I'm a police officer, sir.' The last word scourged his gullet, but it was instantly effective.

'Have you discovered who nabbed my rifle?'

McLevy seated himself, with his notebook on his knee, observing the sparse chin hair that sprouted from a crop of pimples. He held up his pencil. Lying to this arrogant boy would be a pleasure.

'Remind me of the details, sir.'

The youth groaned. '*Again?* When we set out I had a gillie to carry my gun, and then I thought, hold on, he might damage it, so I told the native to give it back. Didn't examine it. Not the thing when talking to a lady, eh?' He gave a leer.

Sixteen, perhaps going on seventeen. McLevy lowered his head.

'Later I saw it *wasn't* my gun. I turned back and caught the gillie halfway back to the house. Or one of them.' The voice became doubtful.

'Anyway, my rifle wasn't in the gun room. Only its case. I had to grab one from the rack. They say I got a royal straight through the head. Pretty good, eh, with some other chap's gun?'

A fatherly lie, no doubt, but McLevy could not bring himself to crush such fragile self-esteem. There wasn't much to be gained in prolonging this interview. He wondered how he could obtain a look at the gun found in the woods, and began to fold his notebook.

'Congratulations, sir. I dare say your rifle will turn up somewhere at Kilcorrie.'

The youth retorted petulantly. 'Don't your superiors tell you chaps anything? It's turned up in the taproom. Now you've got to find out who pinched it.'

From a corner of the room he brought over a long leather box, which he unclasped with a reverential air.

McLevy gazed into the gun case. The smooth embrace of barrel and stock spoke of hours of expert shaping, not to mention a price equivalent to several years of his own pension. He had seen it before: on Thursday night, standing against the wall behind Jack Douglas.

He knew the answer before he asked the question. 'Is this an Express rifle?'

Young Maxwell put his hands into his pockets and lounged against the windowsill. 'The father bought it for the tinchel. Funny thing, constable, I handed over that antique blunderbuss to the gillie chap, but Hatterton and his merry band found it near the place where Enderby was shot.'

McLevy remembered something from his conversation with Dr Sandy, and had a premonition of disaster.

'So this other gun – whose was it, sir?'

'How should I know? He had his initials carved on the stock. *D Mac* – something like that.'

The door of the parlour opened. Mrs Gregory brushed past the youth and cried in a distraught voice, 'Mr McLevy, please speak to the fiscal. They're going to arrest Donald for killing Mr Enderby!'

Chapter Twenty

McLevy abandoned young Maxwell in the parlour, asking as he followed Mrs Gregory to the kitchen, 'Does Donald's brother know that he's to be charged?'

'The minute the fiscal finished with him Hector was off to his millstone. The three others went as well.' They had set out almost two hours before, at half past eight, said Mrs Gregory. By now the stone would have been brought down to Corrie mill.

McLevy hurried off to find Hector.

He was alone in the main chamber of the mill, beating his right fist slowly on the upper grinding stone. As McLevy picked his way over the chaff-strewn floor Hector swung round.

'Four of us, and we couldn't set it straight! I'll have to send for Jimmy Dewar.'

'There is a knack in fitting a millstone, I suppose.'

He was amazed that Hector could still be so absorbed in his private concerns. Yet wasn't it this very obsessiveness which made him a suspect for Mr Enderby's murder? He had worsened his family's plight by his defiance, and even now he looked as ready to brim over as a boiling pot.

'Mr McIver, your brother is about to be charged with the murder of Mr Enderby.' McLevy watched closely to see the effect of his news.

There were the expected responses of shock, disbelief,

and alarm. If Hector felt any guilt, he hid it well.

'On what grounds has Donald been accused?' He sounded bewildered rather than indignant.

McLevy said, 'His gun was hidden near the place where you discovered the body.'

Hector cried incredulously, 'Donald could not have killed Mr Enderby with that gun!'

The remark was revealing, but McLevy had no time to think about it; he was trying to keep up with Hector as they ran back to the Dunfillan Arms.

Mr Maxwell agreed to see Hector; their conversation lasted half an hour. Hector did not return to the kitchen afterwards, but rushed out of the inn with a look of contorted anguish. He was trying to shield his face with his cap. Ten minutes later, Donald was formally arrested.

There was a small crowd standing outside the Dunfillan Arms when the policemen emerged with Donald handcuffed between them.

McLevy moved to block the view from the kitchen window. It was unnecessary; Mary was sobbing uncontrollably with her head on the table, not even aware that Donald was being taken away.

The young man was helped up to the trap, where he sat with his eyes turned away from the inn. Two vehicles filled up with policemen and court officers. Donald had still not looked round when they disappeared round a bend of the road to Dunfillan.

McLevy did not believe the evidence about the gun could stand up to examination; yet sometimes the law made appalling blunders. He tried to remember when the winter circuit of the High Court arrived in Perth.

As McLevy continued gazing out of the window, Mrs Gregory clasped his arm.

'Will you have a word with the fiscal yourself?'

He did not think it would do much good, apart from relieving the women's anxiety, but he agreed, and went once more to the hall. One of the sheriff's officials had been left behind; he was packing ink and pens into a portable writing desk.

'May I speak to Mr Maxwell?'

The clerk nodded towards the parlour door. Inside, the fiscal was relaxing over a bottle of madeira and some sandwiches.

'Oh, it's you, McLevy.'

'I take it that Mr McIver was not able to convince you of his brother's innocence.'

'That is not an appropriate question.' The fiscal gave a quizzical smile over his pince-nez.

'Sir, young McIver's gun could not have fired an Express bullet.'

The fiscal put his feet on the table and munched a sandwich.

'Look here, McLevy, Dr McLaren is a good general physician, but forensic is beyond him. To claim he can tell it was an Express rifle!'

'You agree that Mr Enderby was killed with a rifle?'

'Oh yes. If the weapon we found had been a shotgun that would be different. I would trust Dr McLaren not to overlook lead pellets.'

'The evidence against Donald McIver is not even circumstantial.'

The fiscal pushed the sandwiches over to McLevy. 'These are excellent... McIver admits he walked home through the woods at seven o'clock and that the rifle is his. It was hidden within thirty yards of the body.'

Even if the fiscal could be persuaded that Mr Enderby had been killed with his son's Express that still wouldn't exculpate Donald, who could have stolen the gun and later deposited it at the inn. The same argument applied to Hector. Despite this, McLevy persisted.

'If it turns out that Donald McIver is innocent – '

'The charge will be dismissed. Enderby might have been

shot by a poacher or someone distilling illicit whisky. I've asked the chief constable to have the whole glen searched.'

McLevy felt powerless. His fingerhold on the case would vanish if he protested too strongly that the arrest had been premature.

After pouring another glass of madeira, the fiscal said, 'Someone may have seen Enderby after he left the tenants' dinner.'

'Or be able to give a precise time for the shot.'

Mr Maxwell shook his head. 'No, I spoke to Brodie before leaving Kilcorrie. Many of the guests returned late from the tinchel and emptied their guns near the house.'

McLevy wondered if the message he had brought had mentioned the mutilation of Mr Enderby's body. He fancied not; but he would leave Dr Sandy to deal with that.

Mr Maxwell smacked his lips over the madeira. 'I think I've already run a few important facts to earth.'

McLevy waited. Few men preferred being discreet to the glorification of their own cleverness.

'I was impressed with Hector McIver's good sense during my first examination; but not this time. He mumbled and seemed quite out of countenance. Of course, he's changed into his working clothes; but it was what he said that made young Donald's guilt more probable.'

'Why, has he incriminated him?'

'He told me that it was he who hid the gun in the woods yesterday afternoon. He intended to place some game beside it, to involve his brother in a poaching charge. I asked what game. Grouse, he said, or a hart from the deer larder.' Mr Maxwell laughingly dabbed at his mouth with a handkerchief.

McLevy had heard that the head keeper at Kilcorrie was in general charge of the estate during Mr Enderby's absence. He said, 'Is it likely that Donald would shoot his employer a few months before being promoted? And he is to be married in March.'

Maxwell twirled his glass against the light. 'After one cock-and-bull story, Hector McIver concocted another.'

'About hiding the gun?'

'Worse – his reason for doing so. He says he's been in love with Donald's sweetheart for nearly ten years, and wants him out of the way so that he can marry her himself.'

McLevy had a vivid memory of the scene between Hector and Mary Gregory on his first evening in Glencrannich.

'Is that so impossible?'

'Pshaw! The lassie is bonny enough, but McIver is too sensible to marry a girl from a taproom. He is well educated and was meant for a higher place in society. The whole thing is a fabrication.'

McLevy gripped the edge of the table. The fiscal's complacency was beginning to irk him. 'Why should Hector make up such a story, sir?'

'It's a misguided attempt to help his brother. The usual Highland clannishness. Or worse. Before that, I was hesitant about agreeing to his brother's arrest.'

McLevy thought that if there was any concealment it lay the other way round. He had to speak out.

'Hector McIver nursed a deep grudge because he and his family were to be evicted next May. Yesterday he heard that the date was to be advanced to November. He arrived at Kilcorrie House at half past eight in the evening, demanding to see Mr Enderby. His shortest route was to walk through the woods.'

Mr Maxwell's feet left the table. At another time McLevy would have relished his consternation. He repeated what the gamekeeper had told him.

Trying to hide the impact of McLevy's information, the fiscal said, 'I'll put off Donald's committal for a few days while we investigate further. Meantime you are not to repeat this to anyone, McLevy.'

'Sir, Mary Gregory is deeply distressed, and so is her mother.'

'The family is affected whichever of them did it. This way we may spring the older brother. He seems to have a troubled conscience. At least Donald's arrest will take this pack of hyenas off our back.'

Several news writers had travelled on the early train with the policemen and sheriff's officers.

'What about Mrs Vesey, sir?'

'I shall have to look into her death as well, but I expect it to remain an unsolved mystery.'

So he too believed that Mr Enderby had killed Abby.

'Will you speak to Dr McLaren about his report?'

'If he's still at Kilcorrie. I have to call on Mrs Enderby later this afternoon to offer my condolences.'

McLevy went to collect Jeanie Brash from the stable yard. He must not waste too much energy on cursing Mr Maxwell. He went upstairs and lay down with the dog curled over his ankles. Gone were the days when he could work on a case for two days and nights without rest.

At one o'clock he awoke, put on his boots, and went downstairs by the visitors' staircase. It squeaked under his weight, attracting a turn of the head from a tall, grey-bearded man who was standing at the front door with his hands in his pockets. The man advanced towards him.

'Sir, I am Charles Clark, solicitor to Mrs Melton, a relation of Captain Hatterton. I hear that you are investigating this terrible affair at Kilcorrie House.'

'Not officially, Mr Clark. How may I help you?' McLevy had to stifle a touch of impatience. He was anxious to begin his search.

'I must not intrude on the family in its grief, but I need to speak to Captain Hatterton about some legal documents. Shall you be visiting Kilcorrie in the near future?'

McLevy came sharply to attention. How could Charles Clark have missed the captain earlier that morning? This approach must have some purpose. He had a firm belief in his own good luck; the opportunity was seized.

'As it happens I am on my way there. Shall I convey your request to Captain Hatterton?'

Mr Clark grasped his hand vigorously. 'My dear sir! Captain Hatterton left in great haste last Thursday to travel to Edinburgh, and I was unable to verify some dates given to me by his godmother. Mrs Melton's imprecision in all matters relating to the calendar is well known. Between ourselves, I fear this may be a family trait.'

His eyes held the other's in open complicity.

In his hurried departure Jimmy Dewar had left half a venison patty in the bedroom. As McLevy mounted the wooded slope behind the inn he shared it with Jeanie Brash.

The path rose steeply towards the peat road that ran along the top of the ridge. The outcrop of rock was easy to find; from the scattered chippings he located the exact site where Jimmy Dewar had cut the millstone. The heavy disc had gouged a rut in the ground as it was pushed towards Kilcorrie.

Almost as soon as he began to follow this along the peat road McLevy caught a whiff of paraffin; on the right-hand side of the track coloured lanterns similar to those on the façade of Corrie Castle had been placed at ten-yard intervals. One of them was still alight, but as he picked it up the flame expired in oily smoke. Whoever had put the lanterns there must have expected the path to be used on Thursday evening.

The track continued to rise until he reached a point where the ground dipped steeply towards Mr Enderby's parkland. Here it zigzagged over a tangle of exposed tree roots, the earth between them puddled into mud from last night's rain.

He left the track for the soft carpet of leaf mould, cautiously prodding his way downwards with a length of branch. There was a trail of gashed tree trunks where the stone had broken loose and run downhill. The devastation extended almost to the boundary of the wood. The stone had finally been halted by the trunk of a fallen beech tree.

McLevy examined the ground. Captain Hatterton's party had evidently found the gun before they reached the tree; they had stopped turning over the layers of copper leaves about thirty yards away from it. Beside the prone trunk was a pile of thrown-up earth where the millstone had been pulled off Mr Enderby's body. Between these two points there was hardly any disturbance except that caused by Hector and his companions when they rolled the millstone down to the glen road.

The murderer would not have been stupid enough to throw away the cartridge case so near the body, thought McLevy. Nevertheless he searched around, after tethering Jeanie Brash, who was helping too enthusiastically.

Fifteen minutes later he discovered not a cartridge case but something much more significant. He wrapped the object in a handkerchief before stowing it in his deepest pocket. It would produce a sensation in court; yet unless he could narrow the list of suspects, he might as well throw it away.

Chapter Twenty-one

A black carriage was standing on the gravel sweep outside Kilcorrie House, revealing by a line of small gilt lettering that it belonged to a firm of funeral directors in Dunfillan. The lozenge of Mr Enderby's hatchment had already been nailed above the front door.

McLevy removed his hat as he stepped under the porch to pull the door bell. Flora McLaren answered his ring.

'How glad I am to see you, Mr McLevy! We have been plagued by writers from the daily journals. I am guarding the door myself.'

Although the sun shone brightly the light inside the hall was much dimmer than earlier in the day. A man with a ladder was moving round the galleries with two maid-servants, swathing the walls in black.

McLevy put his request after telling Flora that Donald McIver had been arrested for Mr Enderby's murder.

'Mrs Enderby will be sorry to hear this, but you must wait until after the funeral to question her.'

McLevy began to march the brim of his hat between his fingers, another habit which his sister had tried to suppress.

'The police officers will have no such scruples. I may be able to spare her some discomfort.'

Not strictly true; but when the trail was hot his conscience did not twinge over niceties.

Flora mounted the stairs. Ten minutes later she returned to say that Mrs Enderby had agreed to meet him in the library.

'She has stipulated that I should be present.'

He was vexed, but did not see how he could refuse. Flora took him upstairs and said she would bring Mrs Enderby in a few moments.

The site of their meeting confirmed McLevy's assurance that his good luck would hold. He had a strong conviction that the library had something to tell him.

The bookshelves extended across only two ends of the vast room. They were filled with volumes that looked as if they had never been taken down. In one corner was a stair that led downwards to the ground floor. At least sixty sets of deer antlers were ranged above the windows, although only a dozen vaunted their full number of points. Mr Enderby must have been an ardent stalker. The horns were all attached by their skull plates to plain oak shields. None had been mounted with its head.

McLevy gazed up at these and then walked around the billiard table. He searched for and found an unmended tear in the green baize near one of the pockets.

The southern windows overlooked the park; to the north they faced the beech and larch plantations behind the peat road. Three elephantine oak tables stood in window bays, each supplied with stands of writing paper and envelopes. Beside these were crystal inkwells set into elaborate bronze stands. The ink had long since dried up.

Behind each inkwell was a shallow jar holding a steel pen, the nibs plunged into an inch or so of shot. McLevy pulled one out; it was corroded with rust. As he was replacing the pen his eye was caught by a coloured gleam among the tiny lead pellets. He extracted an oval wafer of gold set with an onyx carved with a lion's head. This was not what he was looking for, but it was a bonus. McLevy smiled and put the seal into his pocket as Mrs Enderby entered the room with Flora.

Mrs Enderby went to sit by the chimney-piece. She was wearing a magenta-coloured gown and a black shawl drawn over her shoulders. With a wan smile she pointed at the chair opposite. Flora retreated further into the room, where she begin turning over the *Illustrated London News*.

There was a slackness about Mrs Enderby's features that suggested total exhaustion.

'I shall not keep you long from Mrs Hatterton, ma'am.'

Mrs Enderby gave him a look of puzzled irritation. She seemed to have difficulty in holding her eyes in focus. 'I have asked Mrs Frazer to sit with my daughter.'

McLevy recalled an incident last winter when he had been walking with Jeanie around Duddingston Loch. She had rushed to the water, found it solid, and scampered to the middle. The ice was thawing; he heard it creak beneath her. Twenty feet from the bank she crouched in paralysed terror. McLevy stepped towards her with whispers of encouragement. He had been almost as terrified himself. It seemed several hours before Jeanie crept back to the frozen reeds. His throat had pained him for a week.

Now he had the same sense of treading across dangerous ice. He began by asking Mrs Enderby when she had last spoken to Abby Vesey.

'We exchanged our last remarks at the wedding breakfast.'

'Would you not expect Mrs Vesey to help you prepare for the ball, ma'am?'

Mrs Enderby's head lifted slightly. The level voice was strikingly at odds with the tremulousness of her face. 'Abby acted as lady's maid to my daughter, not to me. She was more of a friend than a servant. I didn't expect her to stay by my side. If only she had!'

He asked what she had done after the wedding breakfast, and was told she had gone to rest in her bedroom.

'Were you there all afternoon?'

'No, I rose when the clock struck half past two and

dressed. Then I went downstairs and talked with the other ladies in the garden. For a while we watched the girls at their archery, and afterwards we went indoors for tea. Abby was already lying dead in that –' She fell silent.

McLevy waited a few seconds. 'When was the last occasion you saw your husband?'

Her voice harshened. 'I caught sight of him walking along the path beside the wood, not long after half past two.'

If that was true, Mr Enderby could not have killed Abby Vesey. 'So you did not meet your husband after the tinchel?'

'Why should I? After tea I spent some time with my housekeeper, Mrs Frazer, and then I prepared for the ball.'

'When did you last *speak* to Mr Enderby?'

'Yesterday, before he left for the tinchel.'

She had been drawing a lace handkerchief through her fingers; now she let her hands fall to her lap and gave McLevy a hostile look. 'We were talking about family matters.'

McLevy returned his smoothest, most sympathetic smile. 'Ma'am, Mr Enderby's own death does not alter the fact that he disappeared after an unexplained murder.'

For the first time he had her full attention. 'Mr Enderby had not quarrelled with Abby, if that is what you are implying. They were good friends. In fact, at one time –' This train of thought was quickly censored. 'Our conversation was about something else. I was angry at being misled.'

He could see the struggle with her sense of decorum. Flora walked over and pressed Mrs Enderby's hands.

'Rose, my dear, you may feel more at ease if I leave you alone with Mr McLevy.'

For this heroic self-denial McLevy thought better of the doctor's sister; but he was dismayed at the interruption. However, Mrs Enderby did not even look at Flora. Leaning forward, she pulled the shawl across her plump bosom. 'It was I who quarrelled with Abby, not Mr Enderby. She kept saying the marriage wasn't regular. I said not to be so silly. I didn't twig till later. They lied to me, Mr McLevy!'

Her voice had lost its precision; the curdled trills of east London were rising thick as cream.

'I thought Scotch marriage meant larking off to Gretna Green. This was like a church wedding in England, they told me, only in the house. It wasn't, though. It can't be without the banns. There was no service, no taking their vows, not anything. Abby was right.'

A most ingenious fudge, Dr Sandy had remarked on the way to Kilcorrie.

'When did Mrs Hatterton travel to Glencrannich, ma'am?'

'The tenth of August. I thought it would be a proper marriage, not just saying in front of witnesses you're married, then off to the sheriff and get regulated! It isn't Christian!' She began to weep.

He wanted to be sure that he was not mistaken. 'Are you saying that Mr Enderby and your daughter knew that the marriage was irregular – and the bridegroom as well, I suppose – but not yourself?'

'That's right, everyone except me! It all came out at the wedding. If you can call it that! I couldn't speak out, could I? Not in front of all those nobs.'

McLevy remembered what he had seen in the stifling atmosphere of the marquee. He must press the advantage before her husband's death sank in.

'Was your last conversation with Mr Enderby only about the marriage?'

'I told Harry what I thought of him, and he walked his chalks. He knew he was in the wrong.' The words slurred wearily.

'Their union is perfectly legal, if that is what concerns you, Mrs Enderby.'

'Not until they've seen the sheriff,' she fretted.

'The legality is retrospective, provided the couple declare themselves within three months. Why didn't you wait to have the banns called in the usual way?'

'It takes six weeks down here, doesn't it?' Her voice was beginning to regain its usual inflections.

'Yes, ma'am, but I was asking about your personal reasons. Why should Mrs Hatterton be married in three weeks' time, rather than six?'

She said defensively, 'I had to see Alice's gown finished before I came down from London. I couldn't spend another six weeks at Kilcorrie before the wedding.'

How long would it take a fashionable dressmaker to fit and sew a wedding gown? Surely not so long that Alice Enderby couldn't reside at Kilcorrie for the necessary month and a half? She had already preceded her mother by over a fortnight. The answer came to McLevy as if spoken aloud. He hoped it did not show on his face. He picked up his hat and excused himself.

Glancing round from the doorway, he saw that Mrs Enderby had already forgotten their conversation. She was oblivious to her surroundings; her knuckles were pressed into her mouth in a gesture identical with Mrs Vesey's when she spoke to Henry Enderby before the tinchel.

He must wait until proof was irresistible. It would be unpardonable to blast the young woman's chastity on mere presumption. Mrs Enderby was concealing something, but it wasn't the fear that Alice had conceived a child before her wedding.

Chapter Twenty-two

It was now half past three, and McLevy went to the front door to gaze across the parkland. The undertaker's carriage had been driven away, and there was not a single person or vehicle in sight. The only movement came from two swallows wheeling at a vast height in the dappled sky. The Enderby murders were expanding into a similarly infinite perspective.

There was someone else to be interviewed; and he must go to Perth in search of the elusive Mairi. Apart from the killer she must be the last person who had seen Mrs Vesey alive.

McLevy remembered that he had not passed on Mr Clark's message. He collected Jeanie from the kitchen and asked a young footman where he might find Captain Hatterton. He was directed to the kennels.

Miles was crouched between the two deerhounds, rubbing their paws with whisky. He looked up.

'No one saw to them yesterday. Too much excitement.'

'Excitement, sir?'

'I meant the ball.'

His lugubrious look seemed artificial and he reddened under McLevy's gaze. The detective reminded himself that young people found it hard to mourn for their elders. Their own bodies were pulsing with fresh red blood; they were impatient with death. He'd heard that Miles had been decorated for bravery in the Crimea. He was used to sudden losses, but might be uncomfortable with the prolonged funeral rites.

All the same – and McLevy's fingers touched the small stone in his pocket – he would keep Captain Hatterton's seal.

After passing on the message from Mr Clark, McLevy returned indoors and asked whether Dr McLaren was still at Kilcorrie. He was told he would find him in the library. Presumably Mrs Enderby had retired to a private parlour. Again he wondered why she had chosen to see him in that particular room.

The library door was ajar; against one of the south-facing windows was silhouetted a chairback with a stovepipe hat and two boots perched above it. Wisps of blue smoke drifted upwards.

McLevy advanced further into the room; Dr Sandy was slumped in a leather chair, his feet propped on the edge of the billiard table. Although the tip of his cigar was glowing, he seemed to be asleep.

His eyes flashed open. 'You're back, McLevy.'

McLevy described his conversation with the fiscal and Donald's arrest, and what he had learned about Hector McIver.

'That Maxwell's a fool,' commented Dr Sandy in a resigned tone. 'I've sent for Cairns to return from Dunfillan. He will support my findings.'

McLevy decided that for the moment he would keep the facts about the Express rifle to himself. He said, 'Mrs Enderby hadn't realised the marriage would be irregular. She was enormously resentful at being deceived.'

'Indeed! We thought she would be glad her daughter was married at last. She dislikes Kilcorrie, and has come here only to angle a husband for Alice.'

'The news writers were expecting Captain Hatterton to be given a lifetime lease on the estate.'

'Yes, I've heard that rumour too.'

'The omission from Mr Enderby's wedding speech must have been a disagreeable surprise to his wife. Her second that day.'

For a moment Dr Sandy did not grasp his meaning. Then he sprang to his feet; the red cigar tip was jabbed into glowing arabesques.

'You must be insane, McLevy! Mr Enderby murdered by his wife? Oh, you're certainly barking up the wrong tree there!'

'Is it more insane than the suggestion he was killed by his daughter? If anyone in the family committed the second murder, Mrs Enderby had strong reasons.'

'For resentment at her Scotch holidays, and the irregular marriage? Nonsense!'

McLevy put forward his theory about Alice Hatterton. This evoked another splutter.

'Good God, I hope you do not expect me to verify. It is – it is –'

'I do not argue that *it is*. I ask whether it may be. And if so, who knew? Remember that conversation before the tinchel. We both observed Mr Enderby cutting up rough, as they say. Perhaps that is what Abby Vesey told him.'

Dr Sandy had cooled into irritability.

'Even if Mrs Vesey and the Enderbys all knew that Alice was in an interesting condition, I don't see why that should incite any of them to murder.'

'Suppose Mrs Enderby's chief concern was to prevent her husband learning of their daughter's misfortune? Together with all her other grievances...'

'She murdered him to spare his feelings, I suppose! Why should Abby Vesey be killed?'

'For blabbing, perhaps. I should think by Mr Enderby, although it seems improbable he had the time to kill her. Mrs Enderby's grief for Abby seemed genuine. Alice Hatterton may be implicated as well. Why did she not report Mrs Vesey's absence before the ball?'

Dr Sandy was evidently still turning over the previous point. 'By Scots law the child would be legitimate.'

'Would the Enderbys know that?'

The doctor's free hand thumped the arm of his chair. 'Miles Hatterton would never marry a woman who allowed him to anticipate his conjugal rights.'

'The old excuse... You have forgotten Mr Douglas.'

'Worse and worse,' muttered Dr Sandy, his eyes brightening. 'How will you prove your grotesque supposition?'

McLevy smiled inwardly, remembering that glimpse of the doctor entering Mrs Gregory's bedroom.

'I have at least two more, but I should like to speak to Mr Douglas before I return to the village.'

'He went to fish the Breatach pool. It lies just beyond the end of the drive.'

'I shall look for him there.' McLevy whistled Jeanie from the chaise-longue where she had curled herself for slumber.

The doctor said, 'I intend returning home this afternoon. I don't know whether Flora will come with me. She and Mrs Enderby have been whispering together all afternoon.'

They walked downstairs.

'McLevy, I'd be heartily glad if you could pin this killing on someone before the funeral. Enderby's to be buried on Monday. Alice does not know that her father is dead.'

'Three days? We'll not find our murderer by then. Does Mrs Hatterton need to attend her father's funeral?'

'She's well enough to be up and doing,' said the doctor gloomily, 'and she knows it. I told her she might rise for dinner tonight.'

At the front door he said goodbye and then ran after McLevy. 'That's another odd thing.'

'What?' McLevy began to walk down the drive.

'Well – this is only from Flora, mind – when she let

Hatterton into his wife's bedroom this morning, he stayed only five minutes. He was annoyed because Alice asked to set off for Italy tonight.'

'He couldn't take her away before the funeral.'

'Of course not, but isn't it odd for a hot-blooded young bridegroom to be so reluctant?'

McLevy remembered his encounter with Miles that afternoon.

'Perhaps he's afraid he may be left to tell her of Mr Enderby's death. Just the sort of cowardice I'd expect in a hero.'

McLevy walked through the rose gardens and across the park to the Brodies' cottage. He had decided to give probability one more chance.

The keeper took him out to his vegetable garden. 'So's no to get under the wife's feet,' he explained as he held out a turnip top to the pony. McLevy had smelt the family's evening meal cooking on the fire. The garden fence was strung with the dried-out carcases of weasels, moles and badgers.

'Mr Enderby was not killed by the millstone.'

'Aye, I've heard.' The keeper's expression displayed no personal grief.

McLevy questioned him about the visitors' guns. Brodie remembered seeing several Express rifles, but had no idea who owned them. The guns were Donald's responsibility. He had been based at the deer lodge for a couple of days to move the deer herds towards Bealach nan Bo, but returned to Kilcorrie to help the sportsmen before the tinchel.

Brodie's face wrinkled in amusement. 'By jings, and the most of them needed helping!'

'Donald was already at the dykes when we reached Bealach nar Bo.'

'He ran over the hill behind Kilcorrie. It's the shorter road, but steep. The laird didna think it would suit the ladies.'

'*Fleet foot on the corrie*,' quoted McLevy.

'He's that all right,' agreed Brodie, with jealous admiration. 'But his brother's got all the brains.'

McLevy had heard that the keeper was reluctant to give up his post. His lameness dated from a fall down a gully in January.

'Dr McLaren believes that Mr Enderby was shot not long after he left the peat house.'

'That was a quarter past the hour,' said the keeper. 'He left a while before myself. I got a hurl back with Tommy Black. He drove the laird to the dinner but he didna take him home.'

'Was either of the McIver brothers present?'

'No, but the both of them were at the peat house at the back of nine.'

'Who told you that, Mr Brodie?'

'I saw them myself. I didna want to be out of the house again but Maggie said it was more respectful to the laird. She wouldna leave the bairns, so it had to be me. I didna bide long.'

'Was that after you saw Hector at Kilcorrie?'

'Aye, I cried in to ask Mistress Frazer what game did she want for the Friday dinner. Hector was in the kitchen. He wanted to see the laird. I sent him off with a flea in his lug.'

'Did you follow him to the peat house?'

'Na, I had a lift in a trap with the footmen and the servant lassies. I saw him set off through the woods.'

McLevy offered the pony some crumbs of the venison patty that he had found in his pocket.

'Let me be clear, Mr Brodie. Hector McIver made off from your own home about three on Thursday afternoon, and you also spoke to him in the kitchen of the big house at half past eight in the evening.'

'Aye, that's right.'

'The second occasion was very close to the time of the

murder. His asking to see Mr Enderby might have been a pretence.'

The keeper shook his head. 'That's no likely. Someone fired on the laird at the tinchel and Hector McIver wasna up at the dykes.'

McLevy was annoyed. 'Why didn't you tell me this before?'

'I didna think anything of it before. It's only two hours past I heard the laird was killed wi a rifle.'

'Perhaps it was a random shot. The guns sent up a lot of smoke, and they were packed close together.'

The keeper's pride was stung. 'I placed the gentlemen myself. I made sure there was naebody behind the laird or near him, and I saw the bullet spang off the rock and tip his neck. The one that fired must have turned his back on the deer.'

McLevy reserved judgement on this information. He wanted to ask whether the keeper knew anything of Mr Enderby's movements between the tinchel and the tenants' dinner, but Rob Brodie began to limp towards the garden gate.

'You'll need to let me go, sir. I'm to start jointing the deer before my supper.'

'You've taken the carcases into the larder?'

'We lifted them this forenoon.'

So Mrs Vesey's body had been removed.

The keeper's slow, uneven walk reminded McLevy that there was one more question he must ask.

'When you caught up with our party, did you notice Mr Enderby in it?' McLevy had been walking at the front.

'No.' The keeper untethered his pony. 'You're in the wrong about Hector McIver. Goodbye, sir.'

Walking down the avenue of beech trees McLevy wondered why Rob Brodie was now trying to exonerate Hector. Perhaps he had something on his conscience about the McIvers' eviction.

The keeper had noticed Hector and Mr Enderby pass each other on the peat road; Mrs Enderby also claimed to have seen him there about half past two. If both statements were true Henry Enderby could not have had time to murder Mrs Vesey.

So he had reasoned before. Now McLevy was having second thoughts. The dead man had left the yard by the back gate, but how far had he walked along the track? He might have circled back to the house through the wood, killed Mrs Vesey, and then, like Donald, taken the short cut over the hill.

Chapter Twenty-three

Jack Douglas had put up his rod and the case of salmon flies; he and McLevy were sharing a flask of cold tea under an alder. The afternoon had turned warm and hazy; McLevy had removed his tweed jacket, and Jack's bare legs were dangling in the water.

The Enderby murders were still throwing up surprises, and once more McLevy was see-sawing between his instinct and probability.

'It was you who suggested the Scotch marriage, Mr Douglas?'

'Yes, I read up the Brougham Act of 1856. Alice and Miles had asked me to help circumvent his aunt.'

The captain must have found it easy to cut out such an obliging rival. If Alice had taken a lover, Jack Douglas was certainly not the man.

'I find it remarkable that a family of such standing should allow a Scotch marriage at all.'

Jack said, 'Mrs Melton is full of caprice. She told Miles she would disinherit him unless he married by his thirtieth birthday.'

'You have just said he was engaged to Miss Enderby for almost a year. Surely there was time for a regular marriage?'

'Oh, yes, the Enderbys were planning an autumn wedding in London. Then Mrs Melton suddenly imposed the birthday condition in the middle of July. She forbade them to use a special licence.'

'Did Mr and Mrs Enderby know about this?'

'Alice made me promise not to tell them. She asked her father to let her be married in Scotland, and he was delighted to consent.'

'To the extent of allowing an irregular marriage?'

Jack bent forward to rinse his flask in the river. 'Mr Enderby always pushed to go down to Scotland in July, whereas Mrs Enderby wanted to remain in town as long as possible. Alice has been playing her parents against each other since she was ten years old.'

McLevy's eyebrows went up. 'Very frank, Mr Douglas! Do you know Mrs Melton well?'

'I've never met her. I'm repeating what Alice has told me.'

'What was Captain Hatterton's attitude towards his aunt?'

'He found her whims amusing. He said he liked having two birthdays.'

The words were spoken idly, but they induced in McLevy a sharp tingle of excitement. Jack was certainly not Alice's lover. If the captain's own views ruled out high jinks before his wedding, either there must be another man in the case or a different reason for the irregular marriage.

'What is the captain's birth date?'

'The first day of September. That's why it was chosen for the wedding.'

'And Mrs Melton believed it was some other date?'

'There was some kind of confusion, but I don't know exactly what it was. Why do you ask?'

McLevy saw the young man's expression change as he spoke. Jack Douglas was as sharp as a razor. It was unfortunate that there was no other source for the information he needed.

Unless Jack Douglas was deliberately misleading him.

McLevy said blandly, 'It's my habit is to poke into oddities.'

'Why don't you ask where *I* was when the murders were committed?'

'I saw you in the taproom at eight. Mrs Gregory says you arrived about half-past six and got yourself as drunk as a wasp in a beer barrel.' He was gratified by the young man's astonishment. 'I'd like to know what you were doing before you went to the Dunfillan Arms.'

Jack began to dry his feet on the grass. So that he need not look me in the face, thought McLevy.

'I was in the gun room tying flies. About three I went upstairs to fetch my cigar case and ran into two housemaids taking some baggage into Alice's bedroom. I spent the rest of the afternoon walking round the gardens.' His face was morose as he thrust the flask into a canvas bag.

'You mentioned that Miss Enderby helped you in a blanket depot at Shoreditch. When was that?'

Jack switched at the water with a long twig. 'What a bloodhound you are, McLevy! Do you ever lift your nose from the trail?'

McLevy smiled as he leaned back against the tree and occupied himself with his pipe. He knew he had prodded the young man into telling his story.

It was a rambling one. Mrs Enderby and Mrs Douglas had been matchmaking over the tea-table almost from Jack's tenth birthday. That was before Henry Enderby became his father's wealthiest client. Mrs Douglas had been piqued to learn that her son was no longer considered good enough by her father-in-law's ex-parlourmaid.

'Did that annoy you as well?'

'Good heavens, no! Alice was only fourteen, and I was entangled with a young woman in Cambridge.'

Mrs Douglas had swallowed her chagrin, and the two women continued to meet. In the early summer of 1860– perhaps afraid that earlier plans had made their mark –

Mrs Enderby repeated one of Mrs Douglas's complaints about Jack. Alice, missing the sarcasm, begged him to tell her about his 'noble activities'.

'Why on earth do they interest you, Lissie?' he had asked.

'I want to comfort the poor people in the East End by reading Scripture to them.'

'They need practical help, not preaching. I badger landlords to carry out repairs. Sometimes I have to slap on whitening and re-glaze windows.'

Alice's face had hardened. 'We must minister to their souls as well.'

Her adolescent religiosity had goaded him into a harsh answer. 'What makes you think that you are chosen to do that? Don't use me to preen yourself, Alice!'

She had burst into tears; the subsequent verbal abuse must have been learned in remotest childhood. Jack had retorted that Alice was a spoiled, conceited miss who should be set to work in a match factory, there to learn the real meaning of poverty.

The family connection made it impossible for them to avoid meeting; but over the next two years they hardly spoke. They had been reconciled at the marriage of Jack's eldest sister in 1862.

At the reception Alice walked over and took his hand. Her face had thinned down, he noticed. She talked with mature self-confidence, but her manner had become far more wary.

McLevy commented, 'You have remained on good terms with the lady ever since.'

'Yes. We found it ironic that our friendship should grow over the very point on which we had quarrelled.'

The depot at Shoreditch handed out blankets which had been donated by local warehouses. It was staffed by volunteers. When the manageress fell sick Jack accepted Alice's offer to replace her on two afternoons a week. They had to overcome Mrs Enderby's resistance; she was now displaying her daughter on the matrimonial market.

'It's a remarkable thing, McLevy. Alice is quite a different person when away from her parents. Even down here. I wonder that Hatterton doesn't notice.'

After a year Alice had lost interest in her work at the depot. She hedged when Jack tried to question her, and finally burst into tears.

'That was when I first heard about Miles Hatterton.'

They were alone in the shop when Alice confided the details of her romance, and wept through the whole story.

She wailed, 'We may never be betrothed, much less be married! Miles won't announce our engagement unless I give up working in the depot.'

Her voice had resumed that cloying pettishness Jack had so disliked when she was sixteen. She giggled. 'He is a horrid bully when his mind is set.' Then with a renewed surge of grief, 'Oh, I shall die if we don't marry!'

Escorting her back to Palace Gate, Jack mendaciously invented a young woman who was betrothed to a Methodist clergyman. The handing out of blankets could not harm her husband's prospects, he said. Alice was too grateful to take in the gibe.

Jack had made his way to the Strand, an area he had not frequented since his days at Cambridge. Against the blazing glare of a supper room he counted the Enderby invitations he had refused that year: balls, soirées, visits to the country, parties made up for the theatre. Successive doses of rum and water only sharpened the sting of regret.

'And that is where it stands,' he concluded. 'In the past six months the rum has exceeded the water.' Only pride had brought him to Alice's wedding.

They stood up; Jack looked dazed by this plunge into memory. Putting on his jacket, McLevy said, 'Do you know more about those nightmares than you've already told me?'

'Mrs Vesey said Alice always woke up at the point where she lifted a knife and killed her father... That has nothing to do with Mr Enderby's death!'

'Of course not.' If Jack had lied to him, he would use his weakness for Alice to lever out the truth. 'Do you ride, Mr Douglas?'

'Tolerably well.'

'I want you to send an electric telegraph from Dunfillan. I presume your father has access to Somerset House?'

'Yes, he goes there to consult the birth and death registers.'

'This must be dispatched tonight, if possible.' McLevy took out his pocket book and wrote the message.

As he read it, the young man's mouth slipped into a light-hearted smile. An odd response to the base thoughts behind it, reflected McLevy.

Jack said, 'I have some notion what you are after. That's why I let you winkle so much out of me.'

'There is more than one person suspected. This is only part of a larger enquiry.'

Jack's smile broadened disbelievingly.

'It would take too long to return to Kilcorrie. I'll hire a mount from the Dunfillan Arms. The distance is shorter from the other side of the river.'

He lifted his fishing gear and ran upstream to two huge boulders; they shouldered the water through a gap narrow enough for a reckless man. There he crossed with a frog-like leap. After a wave from the other side, he began running through the grass, the fishing basket bouncing on his back. McLevy smiled as he walked back to the road, but more grimly than Jack. What if Miles *hadn't* managed to get himself married by his thirtieth birthday?

Chapter Twenty-four

A biting swarm of flies and gnats pursued David Bisset and his shaggy dun pony up the glen. The minister flapped at them with his hat and stick, but each time, with airy tenaciousness, the dancing cloud reformed. This physical discomfort was nothing compared with his inner turmoil.

The news from Kilcorrie House had sped like moorland fire along the glen. Now his most urgent anxiety was relieved; dead men took no interest in illicit distilling. Yet this might be a temporary reprieve if Hector carried the tale to Mrs Enderby.

He still had to endure the preliminaries to the funeral. Nowadays there were no drunken processions and screeching of the coronach as the mourners staggered kirkwards, bearing the coffin on their shoulders. All but the poorest used a horse-drawn hearse. Yet they still asked for prayers round the corpse on its death-bed.

David Bisset shuddered, hoping that Mr Enderby had been nailed into his coffin.

He dismounted outside the drive of Kilcorrie House. At the gates he leant against the flank of his phlegmatic pony and took a flask from his side pocket. He had a long, slow drink while he rehearsed some of the phrases intended to console Mrs Enderby. He sincerely wished to console her; but the wish was blurred by darker emotions.

When he was eight years old there had been a murder in

his father's parish. He had seen the woman's body being carried along the street, bloated from its winter soaking in a ditch. He had been beaten for standing to watch. What still haunted him was his father thumping out God's vengeance against the dissolute on the pulpit lectern twice every Sunday for a whole year. He had tried to discard such primitive beliefs, but the battle continued exhaustingly inside his head.

Mr Bisset surfaced from his reminiscences to see the postman's gig approaching and quickly wiped off a dribble of whisky that had run down his waistcoat. Once more, with guilty reluctance, he had put on full ministerial dress.

'No a bad day after all yon rain,' called out the postman.

Mr Bisset replied that it seemed to be clouding over. He remounted his pony and jogged up the drive to Kilcorrie House.

The building exuded an almost palpable air of suffering. He hoped that Mrs Enderby would not be annoyed at his late arrival. Her summons had reached him much earlier that afternoon.

He led his pony along the edge of the lawn fringing the rose-beds to the rear of the house. His progress across the cobbles brought Rob Brodie out of the deer larder. The keeper ordered a stable lad to take the pony.

'This is a most terrible business, Mr Brodie. How is Mrs Enderby?'

'As well's can be expected, sir. She's telt us to send off the venison the same as the laird wished... Mr Ogg says the murder is God's punishment for our sins. What do you think, Mr Bisset?'

The minister hesitated. His Free Church colleague was in the same mould as his father, discerning retributional judgement in failed harvests, icy winters, or disease among the cattle.

'I believe the Deity's shafts are less directly aimed than Mr Ogg supposes. Much must be attributed to natural accident or the wilfulness of human folly.'

The gamekeeper nodded judiciously. 'Still, it makes you think, with Mrs Vesey dead the same day.'

'Mrs – ? Oh, yes, Mrs Enderby's companion. I am sorry to hear it. Was there some accident?'

The gamekeeper gestured towards the door of the larder.

'Step inby, Mr Bisset.'

The air was rank with the smell of deer meat and wet hide. A row of haunches and quarters were suspended from the iron rail. A whole carcase was thrown across the stone table, waiting to be jointed, and in a corner lay a pile of antlered heads, fringed with bloodily matted hair.

'Dangling on one of thae hooks, sir. Miss Alice and the captain found her last night. The news was let out an hour ago.'

Vomit rose to Mr Bisset's mouth. He lurched to one of the washing tanks and threw handfuls of water over his face, not noticing that it was tinged brownish red.

'I thought you'd like to ken, sir, before you speak to Mrs Enderby.'

'She was murdered?' stammered David Bisset.

'Weel, she didna put herself up there, did she?'

'That makes three.'

'It's just the two of them's been killed, sir.'

The minister wiped a handkerchief over his mouth. 'I was thinking of another occasion.' He followed Brodie to the hall and waited there while his companion went to look for the housekeeper. His heart was beating in his throat.

So many misfortunes within a few days, as if a vengeful Jehovah were sweeping through the glen! An irrational dread had filled him ever since that Tuesday morning visit from the Irish policeman. He had encountered him again as he rode towards the Pass of Crannich. His presence seemed an omen of disaster.

Mr Bisset heard the swish of Mrs Frazer's gown rustling towards him. He put the same question as he had to the keeper.

'She is remarkably composed, sir.' Mrs Frazer articulated the phrase mechanically. 'I'm heart sore for the mistress,' she went on in a more natural voice. 'And Miss Alice doesna even ken her daddy's dead.'

After McLevy left her Mrs Enderby went to her morning parlour and sat there, quite motionless, until Flora McLaren entered. The older woman knelt beside Mrs Enderby's chair and took her nearer hand. Mrs Enderby allowed the touch for a moment before she withdrew her fingers.

'How is Alice?' she asked.

'Sandy has said she may rise for dinner. I visited her earlier and found her very restless. Miles was with me. I left them alone together.'

'She must not come downstairs until she knows that her father is – is no longer with us. Flora, would you -'

'My dear Rose, such a duty cannot be undertaken outside the family. She must hear the news from yourself or her husband.'

Mrs Enderby relapsed into listlessness. 'I don't know what to say to her. Why can't I believe that Harry is dead? Our last words were so unkind!'

Her face convulsed into tears, but these were suddenly replaced by hysterical laughter. Miss McLaren's hand pressed sympathetically.

After a moment's silence, Mrs Enderby went on, 'When I looked at Harry's body, I thought, Now I shan't ever have to return to Kilcorrie. I feel so wicked!'

'My dear, you have not begun to realise your loss. Sandy says that may take weeks or even months.'

'Who will look after me now? I am all alone!'

'The young people will not desert you, Rose. Once they

return from Italy they will ask you to keep house with them.'

'They have no right to abandon me at such a time!'

'Well, dear, that is for the three of you to decide.'

'I shouldn't have let Alice marry. I might have prevented it, you know, but what else is there for a woman to do with herself? It doesn't seem right she should leave me, when I have put her happiness before my own.'

Miss McLaren smiled forbearingly. She was beginning to feel the strain of her friend's quick changes of mood.

'Rose, should we not be deciding how best to break the news?'

Mrs Enderby lifted her handkerchief to her eyes, although they were now quite dry. 'Did I not tell you, Flora? I have sent for Mr Bisset to support me. We shall tell Alice together.'

When a servant entered to say that Mr Bisset was riding up the drive, Mrs Enderby went to her daughter's room. Alice was reading. At least, that was her mother's first impression. Approaching the bed, Mrs Enderby saw that the book was lying flat on the quilt while Alice herself was gazing at the canopy above her head. She slowly lowered her eyes after her mother sat down beside her.

'Is it time for me to rise?'

Mrs Enderby smoothed all signs of grief from her face. 'The dressing bell has not yet sounded, my darling.'

Alice sighed and pushed her book away.

'What were those vehicles I have heard near the house all day?'

It was fortunate, Mrs Enderby thought, that Alice's west-facing windows did not overlook the drive.

'They were tradespeople coming and going after the ball.'

'Mama, Miles came to see me at noon. I didn't enjoy his visit at all.'

Mrs Enderby forced herself to smile. 'May I ask the married lady what her husband said to her?'

'He came in with Miss McLaren, Mama, and he tried to stop her going away. He was most anxious for me to rise and go downstairs.'

Mrs Enderby bent over and felt Alice's forehead.

'I shall speak to Miles. I am sure he will excuse you until you are stronger.'

'That's not what I meant, Mama. I do want to rise and dress.' Alice sat upright. 'Yesterday afternoon I told Betty to move his clothes and dressing cases next door. When Miss McLaren went out of the room he was quite horrid to me.'

'You should have asked his permission first, Alice. A wife must never anticipate her husband's wishes.'

'May I never have my own way?' Alice's fingers drew patterns on the quilt. 'I wanted us to dine here together, and he refused. That was when he said I must go downstairs. Would you speak to him about that as well?'

'No, Alice. That is quite different.'

Dropping her eyes, Alice said, 'Mama, he is avoiding me. He does not even kiss me. I asked him where he would rest tonight, and he said he did not want us to share this bed.'

A deep red suffused her mother's face and neck. Mrs Douglas's parlourmaid had not used the vocabulary of the streets but she did exchange cheerful smut with her fellow servants. The mistress of Kilcorrie House had no words to discuss an unconsummated marriage.

Mrs Enderby took Alice's hands. Her own were trembling. All afternoon she had been assaulted by surges of panic, much worse than when her mother died. She wondered if she too was going to die.

'My dearest, Miles and Jack and I all know something which we have concealed from you. That is the reason why Miles has seemed so distant. You must prepare yourself for dreadful news.'

Mrs Enderby stood up, and walked over to the bell. She pulled twice. It was a prearranged signal to the kitchen: a maid was to go to the housekeeper in her workroom and ask her to bring Mr Bisset to them.

Chapter Twenty-five

As he walked to the road from the river bank McLevy glanced at his watch. It was five o'clock. There was one more person he wanted to see that afternoon. He must postpone the journey to Perth until tomorrow, and make up his lost sleep. The information from Jack's father was unlikely to reach Glencrannich before Monday.

McLevy was thankful that the heat of the last few days had abated. The green foliage had revived after the rain, and Jeanie Brash trotted to and fro, fetching sticks thrown for her along the road.

He turned up the lane that led to the McIvers' cottage. A woman with her back to him was digging potatoes in the garden. Two russet-coloured hens were scratching and strutting around her as she trod the spade with small, vigorous movements. After half a dozen thrusts she would stoop to retrieve the potatoes and toss them into a wicker basket. McLevy stood to watch her with his hand on the gate, reminded of his boyhood in Armagh.

This must be the eldest sister, Janet McIver.

At the squeak of the hinge she looked round and his heart turned over. She was the image of Rosa. Rosa as she would have been if she had lived a few years longer. He had been a widower for nearly thirty years.

When he advanced up the path the similarity blurred. Janet McIver had that Spanish darkness of hair and eye sometimes seen in the Highlands. Rosa had been Irish like himself, with blue eyes, not hazel. He removed his hat, still agitated. What a fine-looking lass!

Janet McIver rubbed her earthy hands on an apron and came to greet him. She invited him indoors and made a pot of tea before enquiring the reason for his visit.

When he asked for her brother, she said, 'Hector is away to Dunfillan.'

McLevy felt a complex rush of emotion, and was displeased with himself.

'Will he visit Donald?'

Janet coloured. 'He did not tell me. If I could see Donald myself I would ask when is the trial.'

McLevy described the procedure of committal and explained how she could obtain permission to speak to her younger brother.

Janet listened attentively. As he spoke he became aware of her powerful self-containment as well as the likeness to Hector. Her features were smaller but she had the same deeply set eyes. He was curious about whether she resented looking after the younger brothers and sisters. At her age most women would expect to be married. Perhaps she was thankful not to be tied to a husband. What a waste, he thought again, finding the questions he must ask more difficult than usual.

'I believe Hector had a grudge against Mr Enderby over surrendering the croft.'

Janet looked away.

'Miss McIver, I am sure that Donald is innocent. I am not so sure about your other brother.' She gave him an astonished glance. 'My doubt arises from the fact that Hector told the procurator-fiscal a very fanciful story concerning Mrs Gregory's daughter.'

He repeated what Hector had said to Mr Maxwell about hiding Donald's gun in the woods, hoping to bring a charge of poaching on him. He could see she was trying to overcome her shame – probably at discussing family matters with a stranger.

After a silence which McLevy found painfully embarrassing Janet said, 'It is the truth Hector likes Mary Gregory. He thinks no one knows it.'

'And do they, Miss McIver?'

'Donald and Mary do not know. No one speaks of it to myself or Hector.'

Certainly not to you, thought McLevy. No one would dare.

'Why would Hector play such a trick on Donald? Was it because of the millstone?'

'No, though that is why Rob Brodie was in a rage with Donald on Saturday night. Then Donald ran down to the inn and he had a fight with Hector. I was black affronted with the both of them. I made Hector look for Donald at the big house Thursday forenoon.'

'Did he find him?'

'He said when he saw the gentlemen on the peat road he went out of their way into Rob Brodie's garden.'

'That was not until half past two, Miss McIver.'

A half smile lightened Janet's face. McLevy would have liked to see that smile more often.

'Hector was not in a hurry to find him. He went the long way by the drive and he drank a lot of ginger beer, although he prefers the whisky.'

'So Hector did not go to the cottage to speak to Mr Brodie?'

'Not at all. He came straight home after the gentlemen went on to the hill. He was terrible distressed.'

Straight home after his encounter with young Maxwell and planting Donald's gun, thought McLevy.

'Did Hector tell you what had distressed him?'

Janet's voice dropped. 'It would be the same that you

know about.'

'Mary Gregory? Surely he didn't see her at the Brodies' house?'

'It is where Mary and Donald will live after they are married. When Mr Brodie leaves the glen.'

McLevy remembered how the keeper had found Hector McIver beside his porch. On his own visit he had noticed curtains fluttering at the adjacent window. The sash had been open and inside he had glimpsed a large, unmade bed. The agonies of jealousy were one experience he was thankful to have missed.

'So Hector arrived home – when?'

'Half past three it would be. He went to lie down.' She pointed at the box-bed in an alcove by the fireplace. 'I asked had he spoken to Donald. He began shouting at me and pushed me out of the house, then he locked the door in my face.'

'What did you do?'

'I walked to the village, and let on it was to look at the wedding arches in the street, and then I went to Jessie Bennachy's to fetch the bairns. They had their dinner off her for weeding the garden. Jessie made a pot of tea, and after we all went home. Was I not glad that Hector was quiet now! Donald came in the back of seven, and I made the two of them their supper.'

'What time did you arrive home with the children, Miss McIver?'

She knew why he was asking the question.

'Half past five it would be. They say Mr Enderby was killed later than that.'

'Yes, but Hector was seen in Kilcorrie House at half past eight last night.'

'He was inby every moment till the back of eight, glowering into the fire. But he spoke kindlike to Donald, and I was pleased of that.'

'When did Donald arrive home?'

'Not long after seven.'

'Did none of you go out before eight o'clock?'

'The bairns wanted out to the wood, but I was feared to let them because of the shooting.'

'What time was that?'

'Between six and seven, maybe. I asked Donald had he heard it walking home, and he said it was some of the gentry on their road back from the tinchel.'

Letting off their guns, remembered McLevy. 'Did you hear a shot about half past seven?'

'I was in the garden to bring in the washing. Just five minutes it was. I maybe heard another shot, but I am not sure. My mind was on the wee sandy man.'

'Wee sandy man?'

'Yon mason that Hector asked to his supper on Saturday. I saw him in the wood.'

So that was how Jimmy Dewar had met Janet. McLevy hoped she had taken a dislike to him.

'Did you speak?'

'I only saw him through the trees. He looked like he was walking here but he turned away.'

The likelihood that Mr Enderby was dead before Hector McIver left home brought McLevy great satisfaction but this was marred by discovering that the mason had intended to visit Janet. He would scare him out of his wits for such presumption.

McLevy checked himself; he was letting personal feeling corrupt his sense of priorities. His only concern with Jimmy Dewar must be the fact that he had been in Kilcorrie woods at the time when Mr Enderby was murdered.

'Would you swear to all this in a court of law, Miss McIver?'

'How should I not? I would not lie if they had killed the laird.'

'Another Jeanie Deans!'

Janet ignored this foolish compliment, and for the first

time allowed her anxiety to show. 'Have you found out the murderer, Mr McLevy?'

'Yes, I believe I have. Both of them.'

The postal gig was emerging from the pass when he returned to the main road. While he stood waiting for it Mr Bisset rode by on a plodding dun pony and McLevy was engulfed by a swarm of flies. Snapping at the biting horde, Jeanie ran after the pony, which stoically ignored both the dog and its minute assailants.

McLevy called out, 'Have you searched for those lists, Mr Bisset?'

The minister swung round in the saddle; McLevy was shocked by the ravaged face.

'I'll speak about those after the funeral.' He urged his pony into a quicker pace.

A moment later the gig arrived. On weekdays, as McLevy knew, it was stabled overnight at the Dunfillan Arms; but he was feeling lucky.

The postman was eager to talk about the murder. McLevy said, 'I have a new trace to follow, but I shall lose it unless I reach Perth tonight. Is there any way I may catch the train at Dunfillan?'

The driver had a small, foxy face and darting eyes. McLevy watched the prospect of missing his supper being pitted against the excitement of helping to hunt down a murderer.

'I'm no supposed to break my round, but it's the Queen's justice as well as the Queen's mail, isn't it? Mistress Gregory'll give me another beast for the gig.'

'That's most civil of you, Mr Nesbit. I'll mention your help to the superintendent.'

This impulsive reversal was quite out of character; he knew he would not work efficiently unless he made up the lost sleep. He was goaded by a sudden, burning urgency to reach Perth that evening. He couldn't speed the message from London, but Mairi Hamilton's story might exonerate both the McIver brothers. That should please Janet.

Before they reached the village Miles Hatterton drove past them, whipping up the pony as if it was being ridden for the Musselburgh Cup. He must be choking on some bad news from the solicitor.

While the postman was arranging the hire of another pony McLevy persuaded Mary Gregory to look after Jeanie Brash. Waves of fatigue began to swim over him. When they set out again he lay down with his head on the bag of letters collected from the glen. Before consciousness dissolved, a tiny hand knocked at his attention. Some important detail had presented itself to him that afternoon, a detail which connected with words recently heard or read. Something about ... about ...

McLevy fell asleep.

Chapter Twenty-six

The postman stabled the gig at the Crown Inn next to the bridge. It was after seven, growing dark. As he walked up the empty High Street McLevy could hear the murmuring of the river that separated the town from its ruined cathedral.

He went through an arched gateway in the high stone wall to an impressive set of buildings topped with a crenellated tower. Dunfillan was the administrative centre for central Perthshire; these would be the sheriff court and county offices. The police station took up a modest north wing overhanging the river.

The sergeant was the same man who had guarded the deer larder. His two constables were out making enquiries about Mrs Maxwell's brooch. He said, grinning at the irony of it, 'They're after yon fellow who was chumming with you, Mr McLevy.'

When the sergeant had enjoyed his joke McLevy asked if he might see Donald before he caught the train to Perth.

The sergeant took him to a stone corridor with three cells on either side. It was lit by one flaring gas jet. At the far end a tap was splashing into a drain. The place felt damp, but that was probably the mist seeping up from the river.

'The lad himself's no bother. We could do without all the sheriff's people jinking in and out.'

All the cells were empty except Donald's. He was swinging himself to and fro in a hammock with his arms folded across his chest. On a table pushed against the wall was an empty dish that gave out a smell of hot porridge and milk.

The sergeant unlocked the door. '

'Donald, man, here's a visitor for you.'

Donald's head lifted; his eyes showed recognition and then he lay back. When the sergeant had locked them in he said, 'Can you folk no leave me alone? I've telt all I ken.'

'I am not here in behalf of the sheriff, Mr McIver.'

The detective perched himself on the deal table, where the chill of the bare wall was soon striking through his coat. There was desperation behind Donald's sullen bravado. If he remained locked up much longer, the sergeant was going to find him a great deal of bother.

'How are they treating you?'

'No that ill. The sergeant's to light the brazier before he goes off duty.'

McLevy asked to hear everything Donald could remember about the beginning and end of the tinchel. He received a rough answer.

'I've said it all before. Just you leave me to my sleep.'

McLevy hit the table with his fist. The McIver brothers, so unlike to look at, shared the same stubborn nature.

'We have only a few moments. Will you let me help you or not?'

Slowly, Donald sat up in the hammock. 'Aye, all right.'

'What do you know about young Mr Maxwell's Express rifle?'

'Mr Douglas came up when I was sorting the guns. He asked who did it belong to, and said it was shame to waste it on a laddie.'

'What was the mix-up about that rifle?'

'I didna ken it was missing till the fiscal let off his tongue at me after the tinchel. At the dancing Willie Roy said he was holding the gun when I telt him bring out thae big dogs.'

'Captain Hatterton's staghounds?'

'Aye, them. Willie set down the rifle by the kennels, and he said it was all my blame he forgot it.'

'Was the rifle still there when you brought home the deer?'

Donald said he had found the door of the larder locked, which was unusual when there was no game inside. The key was missing. After a search he saw it lying by the wall of the kennels. He had not been looking out for the gun, but he was certain that it was not there. He had unlocked the larder and put the key in the gun room for safety.

'Did you look inside the larder?'

'Na. I was telt take the deer to the terrace for the gillies' dance.'

In that case, reflected McLevy, either the murderer had been in too much of a hurry to hide the key or had dropped it near the larder on purpose. When it was eventually found the loss would appear accidental. That presupposed knowing the deer would not be put into the larder immediately.

'How much earlier than the rest of us did you reach Kilcorrie? I believe you took the deer ponies by the short cut over the hill. We arrived just after six.'

Donald guffawed. 'It's a long cut for a pony with fifteen stone of deer on its back! Did you no see us arrive the same time as yourselves? I ran down the hill to take the gentlemen's guns. Then I was a while ahead of you all.'

'When did Captain Hatterton reach Kilcorrie?'

'Just with myself.'

'He ran too?'

'When we came over the brow of the hill Miss Alice was waving from the trees. The captain said, "I'll leave the rest to you and Willie, McIver." I joked him could he no take the royal on his back to show Miss Alice.'

'Royal?'

'The beast he'd shot. It was a grand hart with ten points. The captain's a right gentleman. He's free with his guineas. No like yon Mr Douglas.'

'Go on with your story, Donald.'

'The captain said – it was to himself like – he'd show Miss Alice his horns soon enough, and he gied a laugh.' Donald laughed himself as he spoke.

'Perhaps that was not meant as a joke.'

'Aye and it was. The gentlemen often talk like yon when they're no with the ladies. They think we dinna understand because we're speaking the Gaelic. Mr Douglas took ill at the captain. He spoke angry to him.'

'Mr Douglas was there as well?'

'He was by Miss Alice when we spied her at the trees. He came running up the brae to us and heard the captain make his joke on her.'

McLevy leaned on his knees and stared at the floor. Pass over whether the remark was an obscene witticism. Jack had not mentioned his walk through the wood with Alice.

'What happened next, Donald?'

'The captain and Mr Douglas went down the brae together. They had a right casting out, but I didna hear what they said. The captain went louping down the hill to Miss Alice, almost as fast as I could myself. I was no far behind.'

'Did you see them walk to the house?'

'I ran past them, but no right near. The pair of them was talking away, but they werena close like. The captain was carrying his gun.'

'What about Mr Douglas?'

'He walked down with the ponies.'

'So, you swerved past Captain and Mrs Hatterton, unlocked the deer larder and put the key in the gun room. What did you do next?'

'I waited for the gentlemen's guns. The rest of the gillies was back first with the deer, then the gentlemen.'

'Including Mr Enderby?'

'Aye, he handed me his rifle. I took it in to clean and then I cleaned the captain's. That was already on the rack.'

McLevy asked whether Mr Enderby had entered the house after handing over his gun. Donald did not know. He had alternated cleaning the rifles with helping Willie Roy to unload the deer below the terrace. After he took Mr Enderby's rifle the other guns had been brought to him by the gillies. None of the sportsmen had entered the gun room.

Donald said he had finished working shortly before seven o'clock. He had gone to the kitchen for a basket of food which Mrs Frazer had promised to send to Janet. This domestic errand had irked him, but he had not liked to cross the housekeeper.

He had walked home with the basket along the peat road and had seen no one in the wood nor heard any unusual sounds. Janet and Hector were both at home. Janet had asked him about the tinchel. Hector had left the house at a quarter past eight.

After shaving and changing his hill clothes Donald had gone to the Dunfillan Arms, where Mrs Gregory gave him some whisky. Then he took Mary to the peat house. He thought they had arrived there about nine o'clock. Hector entered later.

McLevy remembered seeing the elder brother seated on a bench by the wall. He took no part in the dancing, but consumed an astonishing quantity of whisky that seemed to have no effect on him at all.

Mentioning Mary's name, the young man looked dejected.

'Will she be coming to see me?'

'I'll ask Miss McIver to arrange it.'

'Janet maybe better'd no tell her to come. Mary'd just be greeting if she saw me this way.' There was a hint of self-satisfaction.

McLevy heard the outer door of the cells creak open; the sergeant's footsteps rang along the stone slabs.

'Donald, when you collected the basket for your sister, what were the folk in the kitchen saying?'

'Tommy Black, the stable lad, was at his supper. Mistress Frazer asked why did he no wait at the peat house for the laird. Tommy said the laird telt him he was walking home and there'd be plenty light in the wood.'

McLevy stood up as the sergeant unlocked the cell door. He shook Donald's hand.

'Keep up your spirits. I'll pass on your messages to Miss McIver and Mary Gregory.'

He returned with the sergeant to the police office. The two constables were back from their search. One said, 'Jimmy Dewar was seen boarding the train for Perth this afternoon. Tell him, Sandy.'

The other constable turned round in his chair; he was scratching something into a report book.

'His wife says he was reading the *Dunfillan Courier* about noon, and he up and streaked out of the house.'

'Would he see the theft reported in the paper?' asked McLevy.

'Na, it wasna put in.'

'I've sent a telegraph to Perth with Jimmy's picture,' said the sergeant. 'We'd be obliged if you'd cast around for him while you're there.'

McLevy glanced at the clock on the wall. He re-buttoned his coat which he had unfastened in the sulphury heat of the office.

'I'll keep a watching eye for you, Sergeant.'

Chapter Twenty-seven

The dining-room was silent except for the clink of knives and forks on plates and an occasional hiss from the candles. There were only three of them, all sitting at one end of the table: Jack, Miles Hatterton, and Mrs Enderby. Jack entered late after his ride to Dunfillan. The servants brought in the dishes, but were told to let the diners serve themselves.

Another place had been laid and was unoccupied. Apart from necessary remarks, there was no conversation.

When the meal was almost over the door of the dining-room opened; Miles jumped to his feet.

'Alice!' You said you would remain upstairs.'

The others were in black; Alice was wearing summer muslin. Her face was pale and swollen.

'I don't enjoy being left to my own company, Miles.'

Her husband reddened; he moved round the table, filling her plate. Alice ate while the others watched her. They seemed anxious to protect her from their silence; banal comments began to be offered and answered.

When Mrs Enderby took her daughter upstairs Jack edged out of his seat.

'Wait a moment, Douglas. Want a word with you. That will do, Lewis.' Miles signalled to the butler, who had entered to place the decanters on the table. 'Leave Alice to the mater for a bit, shall we?'

'All right.' Jack sipped at his glass and then pushed it away, watching Miles apply himself to the cigars and brandy.

After a few moments Miles said, 'Sorry about that nonsense yesterday. Deuced rotten of me.'

Jack gave a cautious nod. 'Your apology is accepted. I'm a bit of a parson.'

Miles leaned over and thumped his fist into Jack's upper arm. 'I'll have to watch my tongue now. Used to be a bit ripe in the mess.'

Jack said nothing. Miles poured himself another glass of brandy.

'Rotten shame about that young keeper.' Miles put out his cigar. 'Best go upstairs soon, eh? Um – um – Douglas –'

'I wish you'd call me Jack,' said Jack irritably.

'I wish you wouldn't sit on a fellow so hard when he's trying to be friendly.'

'My apologies, Hatterton. What were you saying?'

'I shan't – um – Alice – um – no question of *that* before the funeral. It wouldn't be decent. I'll wait until we get to Italy.'

Jack rose precipitately from his chair. 'Damn you, Miles! Need you speak of such things?' He strode to the door.

'There you go again.' Miles shook his head in mild puzzlement. 'No pleasing you. I'll be ready in a tick. Just wait for me to finish this brandy, old chap.'

Alice and her mother were seated by the fireside in Mrs Enderby's private parlour. Alice had taken charge of the tea-table. As they entered Jack heard her say 'You should not have carried such a burden alone, Mama. We must support each other.'

Mrs Enderby held out her hand for the cup which Jack was bringing her. The movement seemed to need immense effort, and she did not reply to her daughter. After a moment of silence she said loudly, 'I asked Mr Maxwell to do what he thought best about the funeral.'

They discussed the arrangements, but the subject was too painful to be sustained. Jack was waiting for a chance to tell Alice what he had said to Miles after the tinchel. He followed her when she walked over to a side-table and began turning over the pages of a photograph album.

'Look, Jack, that must have been taken on the day you visited us at Brighton.'

She had put some colour on her face, he decided, after wondering what was different about Alice's complexion. Her voice sounded weary, but she wasn't suffering from the same exhausted lethargy as her mother.

'I am glad that you can be so calm, Alice.' *Calm* was not the right word, but it was the nearest he could find.

'You see how Mama is. It helps me that I have to be strong for both of us.'

Relieved. That was the word. He must tell her now, while they were alone. He did not expect her to forgive him, but he was sure that he had done the right thing.

'When did you hear the news about – ?' He couldn't bring it out.

'This afternoon. Poor Mama! She could not do it herself. She brought Mr Bisset to help her.'

Jack felt his throat tighten. 'What were you told?'

'An accident in the woods last night. They did not describe it.'

'An accident,' repeated Jack. He bent over the page of photographs, and felt Alice's eyes on him. He looked up.

'I'm sorry, Jack. I should not have said that, should I? Someone killed my father.' She touched his arm. 'Please don't think me heartless. I wept when they told me.'

Miles joined them. Alice turned to him with a smile.

'Look, dearest, here is a picture of me with two of Jack's sisters. Isn't it strange? I don't recall the taking of these photographs at Brighton.'

Jack left them together, almost glad that he had not had the chance to tell her.

The bedroom was full of shadows. Alice was standing at the window holding aside one of the curtains.

'If this were yesterday I could wish on the new moon.'

A reply came from the dressing-room. 'You wouldn't have seen it. Your windows face west.'

Alice let the curtain drop. She walked barefooted across the carpet to the door of the smaller room.

'Aren't you going to ask me what I would have wished?'

There was no reply. Beyond the door, there was the squeak of moving castors, and a soft thump, as if a boot had been thrown to the floor. Alice returned to the wedding bed and lay back with a smile on her face. The small noises in the dressing-room continued for a while, and ended with a creak of furniture springs. The light which was glimmering beyond the half-shut door went out.

When there had been silence for fifteen minutes, she rose on her elbow.

'Miles!'

After a moment he appeared at the door holding up the waistband of his trousers.

'What is it? Do you want me to put out your candle?'

She sat up and stared at him, although there was not enough light to make out the expression on his face.

'Why are you taking so long, dearest? Are you smoking another cigar?'

'Of course not! I shouldn't wish to be so annoying.'

'What is delaying you? I've been waiting for half an hour.'

'Nothing is delaying me. I have made up my bed on the sofa.'

'Miles, what nonsense!'

He went over to the side-table and picked up the candle-stand. 'I shall sleep in the dressing-room. I told you so this morning.'

'We are married, my dear one. We should sleep in the same bed.'

'That's for me to decide. You mustn't play so fast, Alice.'

'Fast!'

'It puts a fellow off, so soon after your pater's croaked.'

Alice gave a cry of indignation and pain. 'You should want to comfort me, not leave me to sleep alone!'

He muttered, 'It isn't decent.'

'At least lie beside me.'

Miles replaced the candle on the table, so heavily that the hot grease splashed his hand. He swore under his breath.

'Now look here, Alice, you mustn't contradict or tell me what to do. I say it isn't decent for us to share a bed while we're at Kilcorrie.'

Alice pushed away the bedcovers. She ran over and clutched Miles's hand, trying to pull him across the room, but he shook her off so quickly that she staggered and fell against the bed.

'Stop that, or you'll really get my dander up.'

She sat on the bed. 'I shall become angry as well if you won't sleep beside me as a husband should!'

'You're my wife only in name, and I'm going to make sure that you're never anything more. Not after *that*.'

Alice asked in a surprised voice, 'Whatever am I supposed to have done?'

He told her. Half-way through she began screaming. She rushed up to him and spread her hands over his mouth.

'Who said such wicked things about me? Miles, I didn't, I didn't!'

This time he plucked her off roughly and wiped his hands down the sides of his trousers. 'I can't bear you near me.' He waited until he was breathing more calmly. 'If you must know, your precious Jack Douglas told me.'

'That is impossible!'

'Are you calling me a liar?'

'No, no, dearest Miles, of course not.'

'Have it out with Jack if you think he made it up.'

'He – he – oh, how could he say that? Only part of it is true. Not the rest!' Alice crouched on the bed with the quilt pulled round her.

'So you have a different whopper to tell?'

She whispered, 'I cannot remember.'

With an exclamation of disgust Miles lifted the candle and returned to the dressing-room. As he reached the doorway, Alice called after him, 'Please, please, Miles, say you won't leave me at Kilcorrie!'

He turned round. 'By God I'd like to, if the talk didn't come back at me. I'll decide when we're back in town. Don't come near me again, Alice, or I shan't keep my hands to myself.'

Chapter Twenty-eight

McLevy was lucky to find a room in Perth; Friday was market day, and the first Friday of September was given up to the big autumn sale of farm animals. Every public taproom was overflowing on to the street.

He went across town to the Salutation Hotel, where he was promised a bed, and ate a beef pie and apple tart at the common table. The waiter said they'd been run off their feet all day; Thomas Cook had brought in three trainfuls on a Highland excursion.

After his meal McLevy walked towards the river. He hoped to recognise the place he was looking for from the waiter's description.

He saw the spire of St John's at the end of a narrow side-street. The three-storey buildings were topped with broken chimney stacks; there were a few shops on ground level, but on the upper floors the tenements were divided into a warren of separate households. A passer-by confirmed that this was the Kirkgate.

McLevy entered a spirits shop a few yards along the street. His enquiry for Mairi Hamilton produced a smirk from the three men drinking at the counter.

'It's two flats up the stair at number eight,' said the shopkeeper. 'I dinna ken if she's free.'

McLevy left the shop more speedily than dignity demanded. He picked his way over the uneven cobbles until he found the street door with the number he was looking for. Behind it was a stone passage with a stair that ascended into darkness above a weak flare of gas. As he climbed the steps his ears caught the sound of infant wailings, the clatter of pots, and two adult voices raised in passionate dispute.

His first rap was unanswered. He began to fear that Mairi was indeed not free; but she opened at last, hanging round the edge of the door with a smile.

'There's another to cry in at the back of ten, but you're welcome to stop for a wee while.'

That gave him barely half an hour. Glancing around, McLevy removed his hat and took the chair she offered. The well-swept hearth was framed by sparkling tiles, and the room had a general air of bare neatness. Two children lay asleep in the bed.

Mairi sat down opposite him. 'Will you take tea or spirits?'

'Neither, thank you. I shall not stay for long.'

'Suit yourself.'

She rose to light another candle. She had a humorous, attractively open face; its youthful prettiness was beginning to dull. A few years over thirty, thought McLevy. Her red hair was loosened down her back and remarkably thick.

'I hope you're no here to waste my time. What's your name?'

'James McLevy.'

She opened a drawer in the table and took out a broken cheroot, which she pushed into a clay pipe. 'You'll be up for the fair.'

'I'm up to ask you some questions about Kilcorrie.'

The drawer was slammed back into place. 'If you're frae the polis I ken naething about yon murder.'

'There's a lad been arrested who also kens nothing, Mairi. I'm trying to win him free.'

She bent forward to light her pipe from the candle and asked with a smile, 'Is he a handsome chiel?'

'Not so handsome with the leg irons on him. His sweetheart is greeting her eyes out.'

'I'm right sorry to hear it. I'll tell what I can.'

'I need to know what the men of the family were doing late on Thursday afternoon.' The news of Mrs Vesey's death was unlikely to have reached Perth; and he hoped to extract his answers without telling Mairi about it.

'I mind seeing the captain in the yard. That was about a quarter after six, about the time Mrs Frazer asked me to take up the hot water.'

'Can you be precise about that?'

Mairi thought for a moment. 'Mrs Frazer telt me to take up the ladies' jugs just before six. I did Mrs Hatterton's and Mrs Enderby's, and wee Annie did the others. Then I came downstairs to fill the gentlemen's.'

'That was when you saw Captain Hatterton?'

'Aye, through the kitchen window. He was coming to the back door. I took up a jug for the laird at the back of six, but he wasna in his room, so I just left it there. Mrs Hatterton looked into the corridor and said would I come to dress her, she'd tell me when.'

'And when did you dress her?'

'Hold on, Jamie, I'll forget if I dinna tell it in order. When I brought the captain's hot water I heard him and the laird talking. The captain said, "I'll see you later, sir," and he came out of the laird's room, and when I asked did he want me to put his jug in Mrs Hatterton's dressing-room, he telt me all snappish to give it to some other body.'

McLevy had slid out his notebook and was jotting down some of these times. 'It would be about the half hour by then?'

'Aye, the clock struck half six when Mrs Hatterton hurried down the stair. I was fair vexed, for I didna want to bring her another jug. But that's the way it turned out.

She'd been to look for the captain, but she couldna find him outside or in, she telt me later.'

'They worked you hard, Mairi.'

'Aye, did they!'

'Do you know why Mrs Vesey didn't dress the young lady as usual?'

Mairi laughed and blew smoke across the top of the candle.

'The family was squabbling like cats. The mistress rowed with Abby, then the laird wanted them all at the dinner, and the mistress wouldna gang.'

'What has this to do with Mrs Vesey and Mrs Hatterton?'

Mairi laughed again. 'Miss Alice telt me she was feared to ring for Abby because of her sharp tongue.'

'Did she mean her disapproval of the Scotch wedding?'

'Aye, that's it. There was an awfy stir about it in the forenoon, after Miss Alice and the captain were witnessed. Mrs Enderby was fair flaming.'

'Did you dress Mrs Hatterton on Thursday night?'

'Aye, I was rung for no long before eight. She was that pleased with the way I put up her hair she gave me one of her old gowns. It's bonny.'

'Just before the tinchel Mrs Vesey said something to Mr Enderby which caused him great distress. I have to find out what it was.'

'Ach, weel, it'll no vex him now.'

McLevy asked if she remembered what Mrs Vesey had been talking about before she rushed out to the courtyard.

'It would be Scotch marriage again. She said if Miss Alice and the captain was no to be cried in the kirk they should run away to Gretna. We telt her no to be daft. The Act says it has to be twenty-one days.'

'Was this conversation on the Thursday afternoon?'

'Maybe. Abby was on about it all week. She called us all heathens. I liked her, but she was awfy ignorant.'

By this time the cheroot smoke was curling up McLevy's nostrils. He lighted up himself, wondering what anyone entering would make of such an ill-assorted pair of smokers.

'Mairi, try to recall that moment of Thursday afternoon. What were you doing?'

'Me? I was at the sink, washing glasses, and Abby was sat at the table. I asked what like was Miss Alice's wedding dress. That was to keep her off Scotch marriage. The rest were fair sick of her. Abby said she was three hours ironing the dress, it came off the train that scrumpled.'

She stopped and frowned into the candle flame.

'Mrs Frazer didna have a full set of smoothing irons. That's what Abby said. Then she streaked like a cat off hot cinders.'

'Repeat her words, if you can.'

'*I carry round my own set, but they must have been thrown off the train. There's none small enough at Kilcorrie... Kilcorrie.*'

Mairi paused. 'Yon's the way she spoke it, Mr McLevy. She turned all pale, then out she ran.'

McLevy stored the information to worry at later. He was now approaching his most crucial questions; Mairi had begun to glance at the door, her mind already on the next visitor. He began a slow putting away of pipe, lucifers and tobacco pouch.

'I'll add your story to what I've heard from the folk at the big house.' He stood up. 'You went upstairs with Mrs Vesey after she spoke to Mr Enderby. Did she say what he told her?'

'Only she was to have tea in her room. The poor soul was shaking.'

'Were you long up there with her?'

'No more than ten minutes. One of the wall bells rang, twice, and Abby said, *That's the family wants me, but they'll have to wait.*'

McLevy's fingers clung to the door handle.

'Did you notice which bell it was?'

Mairi stared. 'Yon's a queer question!'

'We detective officers have to ask many queer questions.'

'It was one or maybe two frae the door.'

McLevy's fingers relaxed, and he turned the knob. 'You've been most helpful, Mairi.'

'I hope yon handsome chiel wins free.'

He came back and laid a shilling beside the candle.

'This is for your time.' He was rather sorry to see her specious smile of thanks.

As he descended the shadowy stairs there was another man standing at their foot under the gas flare. The awaited visitor, no doubt.

Chapter Twenty-nine

Despite the noise outside the hotel McLevy slept the clock around. When he wakened he was thinking about the Sanders case. He put his hands behind his head and took himself back to May 1860, and the High Street of Edinburgh.

Five minutes later, he sat up with a triumphant smile. The thought that had eluded him in the postman's gig had surfaced. Now he was sure that he knew the name of Peter Sanders' accomplice. Almost as unexpected as the identity was its connection with the Enderby case.

He dressed and went down to breakfast. On his way to the station he called at the police office.

Sergeant Kincaid had regained the alertness McLevy remembered from four years ago. He was a bright-eyed thrush again, rather than the sleepy hen into which last Saturday's heat had baked him.

'Johnnie, I was afraid you'd have been sent to Glencrannich.'

'Everyone but me, sir. Almost the whole county force is there today.'

'Let's hope the peace of Perthshire doesn't fly to pieces before they return to duty.' He passed on the message about Jimmy Dewar. 'You must bring him to Kilcorrie on Monday as early as you may. After Mr Enderby's funeral, we shall arrest the person who killed that young lassie.'

'If we keep it between the two of us ...' The sergeant looked at McLevy hopefully.

'I trust you, Johnnie, but I never cry dinner till the rabbit's in the pot. It's important for the burial to take place first. You must also bring with you the answers to these questions. Can you do that?'

Sergeant Kincaid read the paper which McLevy handed him.

'Mr Liston. Oh, aye, It's just four miles by the train to Luncarty. Would it no be easier to ask right out?'

'You're quite mistaken, Johnnie. Use your discretion about how much you tell him.'

'What if I canna nab Jimmy Dewar?'

'Come to Glencrannich on Monday all the same. I need you for both matters.'

When the sergeant said he would have to get leave from his lieutenant, McLevy replied briskly, 'Mr Maxwell will arrange that.'

'The fiscal at Dunfillan?'

'He owes me a favour.' McLevy laughed, but went out without explaining why.

He made his way to the railway station and when he arrived at Dunfillan asked to be directed to Dr Cairns's house. If the physician was on his rounds, no matter; but it wouldn't come amiss to have an extra bullet for the gun. McLevy laughed again. As he had hoped, Dr Sandy had summoned his colleague back to Kilcorrie.

'McLaren's deduction is correct,' said Dr Cairns, who was home for luncheon. 'I added my signature to the report this morning. But don't ask me to drive there a third time. It isn't my business to find out which Express it was.'

'Of course not, sir. That can be left to the police.'

McLevy could hardly keep the jubilation out of his voice. Things couldn't be going better.

He next went to the office in which Mr Maxwell performed his double function as procurator-fiscal and head of the law firm which handled the Kilcorrie estates.

First he spoke to the senior clerk in an outer room.

'I must know your reasons for such an unusual request, Mr McLevy.'

'They are connected with recent events in Glencrannich.'

The clerk pursed his lips and said he doubted whether Mr Maxwell would give permission.

McLevy smiled and sat down to wait. His intuitions were frequently accompanied by good luck.

Mr Maxwell let ten minutes elapse before coming to see him.

'What's this Johnstone tells me, McLevy? You're asking to see the correspondence on the Kilcorrie estate?'

'Yes, sir. Let me explain.'

As Mr Maxwell listened his face showed even more displeasure than his clerk's. 'That is out of the question. I cannot grant you access to private documents.'

McLevy put on a melancholy look. 'How unfortunate, sir. I had hoped we would not need to read out a detailed post-mortem in court. Dr Cairns agrees that Mr Enderby was killed with an Express, does he not?'

'Yes, yes, McLevy.'

'Then there is the matter of your son's rifle.'

'*Whose* rifle?' John Maxwell's face had begun to mottle with anger.

'The Express rifle that fired the shot belongs to your son.'

After that, it was easy.

Mr Maxwell hung over McLevy's shoulder as he went through the three boxes.

'Why do you require that?' he demanded as one paper was picked out and laid aside. 'It is a personal letter.'

'It shall not be produced in court, and I'll return it to you shortly.'

By the time he found what he was looking for Mr Maxwell was quivering with agitated curiosity.

'This will certainly have to be passed around,' said McLevy. 'As it is of a more public nature, I presume you would not have the same objection.'

'No, but I do not see what it has to do with either case!'

McLevy smiled as he pocketed the two documents. 'No one else but ourselves shall read these before the trial.'

Before he left he also persuaded the fiscal to agree that Sergeant Kincaid would be sent to Glencrannich on Monday morning.

He could have explained everything there and then, but the rabbit was not yet in the pot and he might not have another opportunity to force the fiscal's hand.

He walked into the Dunfillan Arms at half past three. Mr Clark was standing in the hall wearing his outdoor clothes, with a travelling rug draped across the baggage at his feet.

McLevy expressed surprise that the solicitor would not be attending Mr Enderby's funeral.

'I cannot neglect the firm's business any longer.'

McLevy turned to mount the stairs.

'Sir, a word with you.' He beckoned McLevy into the parlour. 'I shall return for the trial, if required, but it is impossible to wait until the police officers make an arrest.'

'They have already made one.'

'We both know that young man is innocent.'

'You do not need to excuse your absence to me, Mr Clark.'

'My remark about the confusion of dates was less than clear. Sir, I shall be explicit. The Enderbys should thank me for leaving the area. What I know about this terrible affair would only bring scandal on them.'

McLevy pulled out a chair; Mr Clark also sat down.

'I am amazed that the family did not postpone the wedding when they learned of my client's decease, early last Saturday.'

'Ah – the day I came to Glencrannich.' McLevy concealed his surprise.

'Indeed? I expected my letters to arrive the following day. They were posted one hour after Mrs Melton passed away.'

'There is no Sunday delivery, of course. This was from ...?'

'York, sir. When she resided in this country, Mrs Melton made her home in York.'

'You said *letters*.'

'I felt obliged to write to Mr Enderby as well as Captain Hatterton. I waited for a reply until late Wednesday afternoon – in vain, of course – and then travelled north myself.'

'Your letters may have miscarried.'

'No, sir.' Mr Clark tapped McLevy's knee. 'Mourning letters have a characteristic appearance. The postmistress at Dunfillan recalled the handling of two such from York. They were sent out on Monday morning.'

'I see!' said McLevy. Those previous hints had referred to the date of the wedding, not to Captain Hatterton's birthday. A pang of dismay went through him.

'I hope you do see, sir. Mr Enderby and the captain concealed the news of Mrs Melton's death. The wedding was held on the day of my late client's funeral.'

'Glencrannich is a far cry from York.'

'Hm'n!' snorted Mr Clark. 'The news of the wedding may not have carried, but Mr Enderby's murder will certainly figure in the York journals. A mere want of respect might be construed as something far more sinister.' He glanced at the window. 'There is the conveyance which I bespoke to take me to the station.'

McLevy said quickly, 'The captain's inheritance was conditional on his being married by his thirtieth birthday. Would that mean *before* or *on* the day of his birthday?'

Mr Clark frowned. 'Your informant is mistaken. Mrs Melton made such a threat, hoping to compel her nephew towards a more sober life, but she relented. The clause was removed before she died.'

'Did Captain Hatterton know that?'

The solicitor allowed himself a winterish smile, perhaps at foibles that could no longer exasperate him. 'Certainly not. I must take my leave, sir.'

When he was alone McLevy stood thinking for a moment. Did it matter that he had misunderstood Mr Clark the first time? All the other facts fitted in. Miles Hatterton had believed that his aunt's condition still applied.

He made his way to the inn kitchen. A flurry of black and tan erupted from under the deal table; with staccato squeals Jeanie Brash leapt up to nuzzle his face. He stepped back from the frantic assault.

'Pack up your fiddle, you daft beast!'

Mrs Gregory came in while he was quietening her. As he ate a late luncheon he described his visit to Dunfillan jail, but prevaricated about the journey to Perth. At this stage it was safer to hold his tongue.

The landlady described how the Perthshire constabulary had invaded the glen that morning, questioning every household. There were six of them billeted in her spare room. So far they had discovered only an unlicensed still above Inverconan.

'And wha among us would ken about that?' she asked virtuously.

Chapter Thirty

McLevy found it hard to submit himself to the pace of the electric messenger. The solution to the Sanders case and the Enderby murders was only a finger's breadth away. At about half past four he set out for Kilcorrie House and loitered so effectively that he did not reach the wrought-iron gates until well after five. He sat on a large roadside boulder and took out his pipe, irritated that he could not control his own restlessness. Jeanie lay down at his feet.

'You're right,' he told her. 'The laddie's maybe taken himself fishing again.' He was hoping that someone might appear to tell him where he could find Jack Douglas. It would have been sensible to make more definite arrangements.

After fifteen minutes there seemed no alternative to the long trudge up the drive.

As he was rising he noticed a sparkle of movement at the side of the house. This turned into the outline of a vehicle; in the still air the sound of wheels and hoofbeats was audible before it was possible to make out the passengers. A moment later he recognised Dr Sandy and Flora McLaren.

Dr McLaren brought the vehicle to a halt in the gateway.

'McLevy! What brings you here?'

'I'm in search of Mr Douglas. Is he at Kilcorrie?'

'He rode back to Dunfillan this morning,' said Flora. 'He said he would stay there until his business was concluded. If you wish, we could drive you to the village.'

Her brother suggested, 'Why do you not invite Mr McLevy to Balinmore? We'll leave word where you are. I shall not dine at the Dunfillan Arms this evening. The place is infested with bluebottles.'

They drove back to Kilcorrie House and left the message ' fell silent. He looked both crestfallen and ill-tempered, McLevy thought. By contrast his sister was frolicsome, or as nearly so as decency allowed. Perhaps she was not so unaware of her brother's amours as he supposed.

He was surprised at the fertility of the upper glen. The road ascended steadily with the course of the river but the Crannich continued to glide through lush haughland set between plantations of beech and larch.

After an hour's driving they passed an arched gateway on the left-hand side of the road.

'We'll go in by the west entrance. You'll see Balinmore before the dark sets in.'

The house lay below in a wide sweep of river, surrounded by fir coppices and harvest fields. It was much older than Kilcorrie, a turretted fortress that made no concessions to modern taste. Across the river the land was divided into small crofts, each with its own slated cottage.

Almost invisible among the heather and tumbled scree, the road ahead dwindled to a track across sheep-cropped grass. The foothills it ran through had the same look as the summits, darkly purple and bleak even in the glow of sunset. Here at last was the barren head of the glen.

'Stand up and you'll see Loch Crannich,' ordered Dr Sandy more cheerfully as he made a sharp turn into the drive through another archway.

'You may find us somewhat gothic, Mr McLevy. We occupy only a few rooms, but you need not be uneasy.

There are neither ghosts nor madmen chained to the wall of the northern tower.'

Flora showed McLevy up a turnpike stair to his bedroom with a paraffin lamp. He found this modern device reassuring; Balinmore was dauntingly close to every child's notion of a haunted castle. Darkness was falling, and from outside came the deep-throated baying of hounds.

'The brutes are hungry. I usually feed them myself,' said Dr Sandy when McLevy descended to the baronial hall with Jeanie Brash slinking round his legs.

'Go and do so, Sandy, before we serve the meal. Mr McLevy and I are both extremely hungry.'

When her brother left them Flora took McLevy to a highbacked settle at the side of a fireplace that could have held a small barn in which pine logs and peat were burning aromatically.

'Sandy is afraid I may extract your news before himself. He usually hurries to the stable yard as soon as we are home. Drink this glass of ferintosh while I am absent in the kitchen.'

McLevy took an incautiously large mouthful and gasped. The whisky was as pale as sun-bleached straw and sweetly fiery. He was left alone to enjoy it for almost half an hour before Flora reappeared with her brother. They took him to a table placed in the least draughty corner of the hall.

The food was served by one elderly manservant in tweed clothing, to whom Flora called out instructions in Gaelic. McLevy guessed that *en famille* the McLarens dined without even this degree of ceremony; he had seen no other indoor servants except a shy young girl who scuttled away when he met her on his way downstairs.

The only wine brought to the table was claret, of a quality that he could not even begin to assess. By the end of the meal, composed entirely of game, apart from a blaeberry pie of Flora's baking – he had relaxed into a contentment dangerously loosening to the tongue.

They moved from the table to the fireside, where Jeanie Brash was dozing beside Dr Sandy's old pointer. There was more ferintosh.

'We were returning from a somewhat fraught scene at Kilcorrie when we met you, were we not, Sandy?' Flora held out her glass. Plainly she did not believe in leaving the gentlemen to their wine.

'What a to-do, McLevy! I fear her husband's death has come home to Mrs Enderby. She is leaving everything to Alice.'

This was so contrary to his perceptions that McLevy had to search for a comment. 'Mrs Hatterton now knows that her father is dead?'

'She was told yesterday afternoon, soon after our departure. Mrs Enderby summoned Mr Bisset to help her. I think she feared the effect, because we were asked to return today.'

Flora added, 'Alice is showing more fortitude than her mother.'

'Superficially, perhaps,' suggested McLevy.

'No,' said Dr Sandy. 'Her self-control is genuine.'

'You mentioned a "to-do".'

'Alice and Miles were avoiding each other.' His eyes moved towards Flora. 'After luncheon Mrs Enderby consulted me as a physician. Her words were so obscure that I am not sure I understood her. I gather – er – it is not the bride who is loth.'

Sipping the ferintosh – was this his third or fourth glass? – McLevy described what he had learned from Donald and Mairi. He also told the tale of young Maxwell's rifle.

'I am now satisfied that neither Donald nor Hector McIver was involved in the murders.'

'You have come to some other conclusion, have you not?'

McLevy's wits were blurred with claret and ferintosh. Later, he was to decide that his meeting with Janet McIver had also played its part. Only one detail was missing to prove his case; he was confident that Jack Douglas would supply it.

'I know who killed Mrs Vesey,' he announced rashly as he brought out his pipe. Before he could search for lucifers, Flora was kneeling beside him with a spill ignited at the fire. She resumed her seat with a siren smile.

Chapter Thirty-one

'The housekeeper's workroom is fitted with its own bell system. On Thursday afternoon while Mrs Vesey was sitting in it with Mairi Hamilton, there was a double peal from the library.'

'Mairi did not say that.'

'No, Dr McLaren, but she remembered that the bell which rang was almost at the end of the row. The bells connect only with the public rooms and are set in alphabetical order – Library is second-last from the end.'

'*That* was what you noticed in Mrs Vesey's room!' cried Flora. 'And the double ring was a device to remove any suggestion that she was regarded as a servant.'

McLevy went on, 'A staircase descends from the library to the back corridor. The murderer persuaded Mrs Vesey to go down it to the deer larder, and there strangled her.'

'Mrs Vesey used to take the family's letters to the hall collecting box. What audacity!' exclaimed Flora. 'Someone else might have been writing in the library!'

'No, the inkwells are crusted with dried ink, but Mrs Vesey would not know that. As you said yourself, ladies do not normally enter the library.'

'An interesting theory,' mused Flora. 'It does not inform us who killed her.'

'Mrs Vesey was so agitated by something she heard in the kitchen that she ran to tell Mr Enderby at once. At first

I thought of the indecorous way the Enderbys pressed on with the wedding after Mrs Melton's death... Oh, yes, Miss McLaren! Mrs Melton was buried on the wedding day. Abby Vesey must have seen the mourning letters.'

He enjoyed their astonishment. 'Yet it seemed far too trivial a reason. Mr Enderby could have found some excuse to satisfy Mrs Vesey. He must have had a stronger reason for killing her.'

Dr Sandy frowned. 'Surely he did not have time to kill her?'

'He could have circled back through the trees. Remember, he knew that Abby Vesey had gone up to that room.'

Dr Sandy refilled their three glasses, and sat back with a sceptical laugh.

'What was his motive?'

'Mrs Vesey was to accompany the Hattertons on their wedding tour. On their way to Italy they would certainly pay their respects at Mrs Melton's graveside. Abby Vesey had a very muddled understanding of Scotch marriage. She seems to have regarded it as tantamount to fornication.'

'And might have said so in York, among Mrs Melton's friends?'

'Exactly, Miss McLaren. She was not a discreet woman. Mr Enderby had squared his own conscience with the irregular marriage, but he had miscalculated his wife's response and probably not even considered Mrs Vesey's.'

Flora said, 'It is somewhat shocking that the wedding took place on the same day as Mrs Melton's funeral.'

'Who took revenge on Mr Enderby?' The doctor sounded unconvinced.

'Mr Enderby himself was killed for a different reason. On Friday afternoon I passed Captain Hatterton wearing a face which might have personified a thunderstorm. He had believed he could not inherit from Mrs Melton unless he were married by his thirtieth birthday, and Mr Clark had just informed him that there was no such clause.'

'Why should that disappoint him?'

'Disappoint is hardly the word, Miss McLaren. To prevent his father-in-law and the solicitor meeting, Captain Hatterton had committed murder.'

Their response would have gratified even McLevy's idol, the French detective Vidocq. The whisky glasses were brimmed again.

'Captain Hatterton was born on August 31st, but Mrs Melton believed his birthday was September 1st, the wedding day. This was unimportant until Mr Clark arrived in Glencrannich. There were papers to sign, and Mr Enderby might be asked to witness a signature. Even Captain Hatterton wouldn't play fast and loose with legal documents.'

'How did Hatterton commit the murder, McLevy?'

'He arranged to meet Mr Enderby after the tenants' dinner and walk home with him along the peat road. They were overheard making the arrangement by a maidservant.'

'In darkness?'

'Miss McLaren, the path was illuminated on Thursday night.'

'The body was found on the other side of the hill,' objected Dr Sandy. 'Even Hatterton couldn't have lifted it more than a few yards. The ground was too soft.'

'I'm inclined to think Mr Enderby was killed very near where the body was found.'

'Why wait so long to kill him?'

'Perhaps Hatterton tried first to dissuade him from inviting Mr Clark to the house. They may have walked some distance before he committed the murder. The place would depend on where he had hidden Maxwell's rifle.

'After the murder Captain Hatterton walked down to the Dunfillan Arms. He left the rifle in the taproom, knowing everyone would be at the peat house. Then he bathed in the stables to wash off any traces of the murder and changed into his evening clothes. They had already been sent to the inn.'

Flora exclaimed, 'What a mixture of cunning and recklessness!'

'The first missed shot at the tinchel concerns me.' McLevy described the attempt to shoot Mr Enderby at Bealach nan Bo.

The mutilation of the body troubled him as well, but he was not going to discuss that in front of Miss McLaren.

Once again a silence fell, which was ended by a grunt from Dr Sandy.

'Dammit, McLevy, you make it sound so probable, yet Enderby could have been killed by a roaming poacher.'

'Or another member of the house party,' said his sister. 'Have you no other suspect?'

'None so likely,' replied McLevy firmly. 'None with so strong a motive.'

'All because Hatterton failed to arrange the wedding for Wednesday! I can't believe anyone would be so stupid.'

'You are looking through the wrong end of the telescope, Balinmore. Men like Captain Hatterton do not plan ahead unless forced to.'

'Nor see problems until they arise.'

'Exactly, Miss McLaren. Wednesday may have entailed some inconvenience to Miss Alice or the family. Miles Hatterton would see it as a piece of bad luck that his mistake came to the fore.'

Flora said, 'I was sceptical about Mr Douglas's ride to Dunfillan. He told us he was having some special salmon flies sent from Edinburgh.'

By now McLevy was feeling quite genial towards Flora. 'Mr Douglas is enquiring for me at Somerset House, by means of the electric telegraph.'

They had been speaking against the soft hiss of logs in the fireplace; outside a mild wind was soughing through the pine trees. A few moments after Jeanie Brash stood up and shook herself they heard a vehicle being driven to the house.

The elderly servant entered holding a lantern. Behind him Jack Douglas was removing a cloak and hat sparkling with rain drops.

'I drove one of the Enderby dogcarts. Your answer arrived late this afternoon, McLevy.'

'It was most kind in you to seek me out, Mr Douglas.'

Dr Sandy handed Jack a glass of ferintosh. 'Now, lad, to make or break McLevy's fantastical notions!'

Jack turned to the detective. 'You covered your tracks, McLevy, but I've had several hours' waiting at Dunfillan to stalk you.'

He brought out the telegraph sheet with tantalising slowness.

'Mrs Melton must have supposed that Miles was born on the last day of August. Here is his true birth date.'

McLevy took the piece of paper. He read, *Captain Hatterton was born on September 1st 1835.*

Miles had indeed been married on his birthday.

Chapter Thirty-two

On Sunday evening Jimmy Dewar decided it was safe to return home. There were three columns about it in the *Perthshire Advertiser* and his name not mentioned once. When he entered the house he demanded his supper.

'You'll get your supper in the gaol, Jimmy man.' Mrs Dewar's anxiety had been tempered by some pleasure in his absence.

'What d'you mean?' growled Jimmy.

Mrs Dewar relented a little. 'Put this inside you before they take you away.'

She then dished up the remains of her own meal. Her husband made some comments about the proportion of meat to potatoes; but before he could settle down, there was a knock at the door.

'That'll be them. Never say I didna warn you, Jimmy.'

Jimmy glared, but bent his head to the plate again, thinking this was some bluff in the matrimonial war that had been raging for ten years.

Mrs Dewar opened the door to admit the Dunfillan sergeant and one of his constables.

Jimmy started to his feet. 'You bitch, Isa!'

'It's no her blame. We've had an eye on the house since Friday.'

'When you were a bairn, Sandy Nimmo, I skelped you for lifting neeps out of my father's kailyard!'

'When I was a bairn, Jimmy, you were an honest man. Come away quietly or you'll make it worse for yourself.'

Jimmy dodged behind the table.

'I didna do it! There was a feck of other folk in the wood on Thursday night!'

Both police officers looked taken aback, and then laughed.

'You surely dinna think we're nabbing you for Mr Enderby?' asked the sergeant.

'What way do you want me?'

The constable said, 'Mrs Frazer at Kilcorrie says you were raiking upstairs when the fiscal's lady lost her brooch.'

Jimmy banged his spoon on the table. 'What's with all you folk? I've no lifted the bloody brooch! You can search my house.'

'They've had a poke already,' said his wife.

Jimmy gave her a wrathful look.

The sergeant went on, 'Maybe a blether with Mistress Frazer will shoogle your memory.'

Jimmy sat down again and scraped round his plate.

'What time are you crying in for me?'

'Nae need for that, Jimmy. Sergeant Kincaid will come frae Perth to waken you. You're to sleep the night at the gaol.'

It rained on the morning of the funeral. McLevy awoke when the gutter above his window, already choked with leaves, overbrimmed and let its water drop into the yard. He expected to see a wall of driving rain outside; instead, a watery sunlight was brightening through the drizzle.

He opened the window and felt a sharpness in the air; Jeanie Brash sprang off his bed and stood with her paws on the sill, barking to be let out. When he took her downstairs she rushed to the strip of grass outside the inn and rolled from side to side, holding his eye.

'Lass, behave yourself or I must shut you up for the day.

We can't be doing with such pranks at the kirkyard.'

The little collie jumped upright and followed him into the kitchen.

'Yon was a long walk you took to yourself on Sunday,' said Mrs Gregory as she ladled out McLevy's porridge.

'You glenfolk have as many eyes as a peacock's tail.'

Still smarting at his failure, he had avoided everyone when he returned from Balinmore on Sunday morning. The hours between Jack Douglas's arrival and retiring to bed had been worse than a public flogging. He could never face the McLarens again.

Why had the case come tumbling round his ears? All the details but one bonded without a chink.

He had opened his mouth too soon, just because of that moment he watched Janet McIver digging potatoes.

The McLarens' elderly manservant had driven McLevy back to the Dunfillan Arms on Sunday morning. They arrived as the church bell was tolling and the congregation moving in through the porch. After McLevy alighted, the driver handed over a small bag of hand-sewn deerskin. A corked glass neck protruded from the top.

McLevy gave him sixpence, and cradled his bottle of ferintosh into the inn.

He was glad that Mary and Mrs Gregory had already left for the service. He wanted solitude to think. He had gone upstairs to sit on the bed. Elbows on knees, hands pressed over his eyes, he rehearsed every conversation he had held in the past nine days, going back to his first words with Mrs Vesey. Among that mass of trivia must lie something to point him in the right direction.

After half an hour his mind was still cold and blank. He placed the ferintosh on the windowsill. It would be both bait and reward, not to be opened until he had solved the Enderby murders. As for the Sanders case, his confidence was now so shaken he didn't want to think about it.

In the afternoon, mindful that to be seen walking anywhere except to the kirk would brand him a Sabbath-breaker, McLevy had slipped into the woods. For an hour he sat contemplating the path of the runaway millstone.

He had then walked along a hillside track that meandered in unsteady parallel with the road, losing count of time. His thoughts had been violently jarred by a high, unearthly shriek that was prolonged in its own echo.

McLevy was jolted back to his surroundings. He realised he had walked halfway to Dunfillan; he was within earshot of the late afternoon express. He turned round to begin the return walk to the village.

After a hundred yards he came to a sudden halt.

It might have been the soothing influence of the golden afternoon, or the interruption to his thoughts. What did it matter, anyway? Now he knew why Henry Enderby had been murdered, and the 'why' explained the 'who'.

His reasoning had been so nearly correct that it had sent him in the reverse direction.

McLevy jaunted along like a lad of sixteen. This was balm for wounded pride. He could cock his beaver again. He wouldn't open his mouth so rashly again, not for a dozen Janet McIvers! Besides, he thought, as the effervescence subsided, he couldn't scandalise Mrs Gregory by such an eccentric request on the Sabbath.

On Monday morning, after finishing his porridge, he said to the landlady, 'Do your visitors ever request any journal except the *Dunfillan Courier*?'

'Oh, aye, there's more than the *Courier* comes to us.'

'Do you keep them by you?'

'Them that's left goes into the coal-house. Kirsty uses them to light the fires.'

'Do you keep them in order, Mrs Gregory?'

'Losh-a-mighty, Jamie McLevy, why should I do that? Is there one in particular you're after?'

She took him to the coal-shed and called for the kitchenmaid, who said resentfully that she had changed into her good serving apron.

'Never fash the lassie, Mistress Gregory. I'll look them out myself.'

In the coal-shed he found *The Times*, the *Perthshire Advertiser*, the *Scotsman*, and several others, all sorted into separate piles. The top copy of each was only a few days old. McLevy lifted half of each pile and studied the dates beneath. He smiled at the girl.

'Kirsty, you're a clever, methodical lass. You shall be my new assistant.'

'They're clarty frae the coal. Shall I fetch a duster?'

'An old tablecloth, if your mistress has such to spare. I must lay some of these out.'

By the time she returned he had extracted three or four papers from each pile. Shaking off as much of the dust as he could, he took them to the room where he had spoken to young Maxwell, asking Kirsty to precede him.

'My hands are somewhat clarty, as you see, Kirsty. Do you lift the fine plush cloth in case I file it, and put down that old one in its place.'

He found the correct edition for all the papers. Although the matter lay outside its usual territory, the *Scotsman*'s account was the fullest of the lot, perhaps because of pride in the national name.

McLevy took out the pocket knife he used to clean his pipe and slit around the column. He put it into his breast pocket with more care than he would have bestowed on a love letter in his youth. He took the remainders back to the coal-hole. There would be ferintosh tonight.

He went to wash his hands before attending the funeral. Through the kitchen window he saw Sergeant Kincaid arriving with Jimmy Dewar. He met them outside the inn.

'Here's the answers you wanted, sir.'

McLevy glanced at the written replies before putting

them away for later study. Some angel of good fortune must be making up for his disappointment at Balinmore.

The taproom was empty, so they held the interview there.

Chapter Thirty-three

The families of the county had sent their empty carriages to the funeral, but few of them attended in person. The procession formed up at Kilcorrie House, led by a hearse drawn by two black horses with dark, nodding plumes. It reached the graveyard at nine. A crowd had gathered from other parts of the glen.

Only one coffin was brought out for burial. Mrs Vesey's had been removed from Kilcorrie at dawn and interred in another corner of the kirkyard.

The family plot, bought two years before, was marked out by granite bollards with linking bronze chains. The grave had been dug on Saturday afternoon. A blank space on the wall behind would hold the commemorative tablet.

The Kilcorrie party, all of them men, assembled at the graveside; among them were the head servants and workers from the estate. Miscellaneous spectators lined the kirkyard wall.

McLevy picked up Jeanie Brash and found a space from where he could watch the faces of the mourners.

The bearers laid the coffin on the trestles by the graveside. Underneath the pall it was nailed over with black cloth, apart from the metal plate. David Bisset raised his hand and began a prayer.

Jeanie's paws scrabbled at the undressed stone of the wall; there was a low-throated whining as she strained against her leash.

McLevy rested her weight on the top of the coping stones. The whining continued, but the dog now cringed back in his arms, making noises of anger and alarm.

'I'll have to take her inby,' McLevy said to the bystanders. He pushed back through the crowd and set Jeanie down on the grass. She shook herself, her fear now forgotten.

'Well done, lass, but your own business will have to wait until after the funeral.'

He took Jeanie indoors to tie her to a bedpost, and then hurried back to the churchyard The brief service was already over, and the crowd dispersing. Three closed carriages were setting off to take the mourners back to Kilcorrie.

As the last one passed McLevy it rolled to a halt. The door was pushed open and Dr Sandy jumped out. He gripped McLevy's arm.

'Do not take it hard, man. You found out one murder.'

McLevy said, 'I have found out both.'

He received a pitying smile. 'Aye, aye, but your proof fell through.'

'Sergeant Kincaid is waiting inside the inn with Dewar, the stonemason. The three of us need transport to Kilcorrie. I want your help to speak with Mr Douglas.'

'Jack Douglas! Surely you do not suspect *him*!'

'You are a magistrate, and can sign a warrant of arrest.'

'For Mrs Maxwell's gew-gaw?'

'For murder.'

The doctor sucked in his cheeks. 'I do not know, McLevy, I really do not.' He glanced at the waiting carriage. A man's face was pressed against the glass, mouthing impatiently.

'I shan't ask for a warrant unless you agree it is necessary.'

Dr Sandy said, 'My dogcart is inside the inn stables. I intended to send for it after the funeral baked meats.'

McLevy smiled. 'Thank you, Dr McLaren.'

'I'll wait for you at the back of the house. For God's sake mind what you're doing.'

'I always mind what I'm doing,' replied McLevy, as Dr Sandy returned to the carriage.

The Balinmore vehicle was wheeled out to the yard and Dr Sandy's pony harnessed to the shafts. While this was being done McLevy went into the taproom.

'It's all arranged, Sergeant.'

Jimmy Dewar lifted his head with a venomous glare. 'You promised no to take me to Kilcorrie.'

Sergeant Kincaid gave a warning tug on the handcuffs. 'None of your lip, Dewar. Mr McLevy said if you telt anything to the purpose.'

'I telt it all.'

'You must repeat it at Kilcorrie,' said McLevy.

He returned to his room and looked at Jeanie Brash. It was not convenient to carry her with him; but the next two hours' events were unpredictable; they might even be dangerous. The little collie's presence would be a comfort.

He drove the dogcart himself at a sauntering pace. The rain began to fall again.

Sergeant Kincaid drew on his mackintosh cape. 'Can you no whip up that beast? We'll all be droukit.'

McLevy fractionally increased the speed of their journey, while Jimmy Dewar huddled into his cloth jacket. He was bareheaded. There was a horse blanket under one of the seats, which McLevy drew out and tossed to him.

'Hap yourself in that, Jimmy.'

He was almost sure that Jimmy had not stolen the missing brooch, and felt sorry for his misery, although it was probably well deserved.

He would have preferred not to arrive at Kilcorrie while the funeral guests were there; but that might mean arriving at an empty house. The house party was to leave immediately after the reception to catch the night mail from Perth.

McLevy took the dogcart to the back of the house. Dr Sandy was waiting inside the doorway. He addressed the policeman first.

'I am a JP, Sergeant. Mrs Frazer is expecting you in the kitchen. When you have spoken to her about Mrs Maxwell's brooch, make out your report and wait for us in the hall.'

He gave McLevy a look of humorous warning, as if reminding him that he would not be easily convinced about the more serious charge.

McLevy said, 'Would you keep my dog beside you, Sergeant? Mind what we arranged.'

'I'll look after the beast,' muttered Jimmy Dewar. 'She's more heart than the lot of you together.'

McLevy handed Jeanie over, with a smile at the oblique bid for pity.

Dr Sandy walked ahead of him. At the foot of the staircase was a mound of trunks, carpet-bags, and other luggage, fenced in by sporting equipment and umbrellas. Beside it lay the two staghounds. Their thin, hairy tails thumped the floorboards as the two men approached.

'Shall I send Douglas to you?'

'Bring him to the library. You must not interrupt even if I seem to bear off course.'

The doctor scoffed, 'I think that failed attempt at Miles has addled your wits. Have you any other orders?'

'Only that you should lock the gun room door.'

'Dewar looks shifty. If we leave him alone with Mrs Frazer he'll run for it.'

'Not if he's plied with tea and whisky.'

Dr Sandy shrugged and went to the gun room. He returned after a few moments with a small iron key.

McLevy stood cracking his knuckles while he watched Dr Sandy walk into the dining-room. The double doors had been thrown open, letting out subdued conversation. Of the dozen or so guests most of the women were seated haphazardly about the room, while the men remained standing beside them or moved to and fro handing refreshments. Dr Sandy spoke to his sister before touching Jack Douglas's arm and pointing towards the hall.

The young man came out in a rush of animosity. 'This is an inconsiderate time to pursue your enquiries, McLevy!'

'May we speak upstairs, Mr Douglas? I know who killed Mr Enderby.'

Jack's face became still. He walked across the hall, where his hand clenched the newel post of the banisters before he preceded McLevy upstairs to the library.

Chapter Thirty-four

McLevy sat in the same chair in which he had interviewed Mrs Enderby. He knew where the conversation with Jack Douglas had to go, but this fish would fight hard before letting itself be hauled out of the water. He took out his pipe and filled it slowly, although he had no wish to smoke.

The young man fidgeted, unable to keep his hands still. He finally thrust them into his pockets.

'Well, Mr Douglas.' McLevy made his voice ironically pleasant, knowing that would act like mustard on burned flesh. 'I have made one false assumption already, so I'll not construct another until the facts draw in as tight as the hangman's noose.'

Jack's face visibly whitened. 'That would seem wise.'

McLevy smiled, and drew a few times on his pipe.

'I know it was not you who killed Mrs Vesey, so I shall not try to implicate you in *her* murder. Mr Enderby's death is another matter. There you share some responsibility.'

'I did not see him after the wedding breakfast!'

'Why didn't you tell me you spoke to Captain Hatterton on Thursday afternoon before you went down to the Dunfillan Arms?'

'Alice asked me to escort her.'

'Did Mrs Hatterton tell you to quarrel with her husband? Something serious must have been at issue.'

He retorted angrily, 'That is no one's business but mine!'

A mere hint would be enough for Jack Douglas.

'The jury would have to decide about that.'

Jack's hands came out of his pockets. 'You shan't lead that as evidence!'

'Well, sir, there's a man lying in Dunfillan jail, and the High Court trying to knot a rope round his neck. The defence may lead whatever it thinks fit.'

'There is no way I can help Donald McIver.'

'Then everything must come out in the witness box. You are an honourable man, Mr Douglas. You would not perjure yourself.'

Jack sat down and stared at the floor, his long fingers twining and untwining. McLevy smoked on for a moment.

'What do you want to know?'

The firecrackers had gone out of him, McLevy noted with satisfaction. He would do anything to protect Alice Hatterton. He was so taken up with his inamorata's situation that he wasn't using his brains.

'What did you say to Captain Hatterton? I promise it shall never go outside this room.'

'I can't tell you. You know I cannot.'

'Then it must be spoken aloud in court.'

There was a final spurt of resistance.

'How can I be sure you will keep your word?'

'I do not make promises I cannot keep, Mr Douglas. Would you let an innocent man swing rather than break a confidence?'

Jack groaned. He glanced at Dr Sandy, but got back only a shake of the head. The young man muttered, 'Hatterton made an indecent remark about Alice.'

'I've already learned that from Donald McIver. I want to hear what you told Hatterton about his wife.'

'I spoke about her illness. I was afraid he'd handle her roughly.'

'You damned namby-pamby!' cried Dr Sandy.

McLevy ignored the interruption. 'What did you tell him?'

He was still reluctant to speak out. 'Something Alice doesn't remember. It came back to her once, two years ago. I tried to consult a mesmerist but I had to drop it. They wanted to know the patient's name.'

McLevy looked at the clock. 'Were you with Miss Enderby when her memory returned?'

'Yes, it happened while she was at the blanket store.'

'Did you repeat to Captain Hatterton what Miss Enderby told you then?'

Jack looked uneasy. 'He didn't take me seriously when I said Alice had been ill. So I told him about her loss of memory, and what happened in the autumn of 1860. Hatterton blew like a keg of gunpowder.'

'Mr Douglas,' said McLevy, 'describe what happened on the day Miss Enderby recovered her memory.'

Jack seemed relieved by the change of question. He does not know my intentions, thought McLevy.

'A few moments before we closed a woman rushed into the depot clutching a fur boa which she'd stolen from a clothes stall along the street. Two men followed her, and when she fell from their blows one of them began kicking her. The other man and myself tried to pull him off. When we managed to stop him, there was blood running from her head. The other man said, *You've done it now, Tim*. We lifted her on to a pile of blankets.'

'He must have cracked her skull,' said Dr Sandy.

'Did Miss Enderby see all this?'

'She took off the woman's bonnet and bathed her head. We sent her husband to fetch a doctor. He was the one who hit her, not the stall holder. *He* kept on saying, *It ain't worth it for a piece of fur*. He blubbed like a baby when she died.'

Dr Sandy cried, 'You kept Alice there!'

'I tried to take her home as soon as the body was removed, but she insisted on scrubbing the stains from the floor. The blankets were soaked with blood, so I sent them to be burned the next day.'

'What happened to the fur?' asked McLevy.

'Alice picked it up. The shop was pretty dark, and I think she didn't know what she had in her hand. I lit the paraffin lamp and saw it was a fox mask with the pelt dangling below. It was still wet from the woman's blood.'

'What did she do with it?'

'She threw it away and asked for some water. The glass was rattling against her teeth. Then she told me about the deer head.'

'Please explain, Mr Douglas.'

At the end of his account McLevy leaned forward. 'It was after you repeated the story that Captain Hatterton became so angry, wasn't it?'

'Yes. Miles was very quiet for a moment, and then he choked. He said, *That shall all be settled in Italy*, and rushed down the hill to meet her.'

'Thank you, Mr Douglas. Will you please ask Mrs Hatterton to speak to me?'

There was a firestorm of protest. The young solicitor shouted, 'I won't let you question Alice!' and Dr Sandy supported him.

McLevy listened stolidly; he let them vent their feelings.

'I must see her, Mr Douglas. It is the only way to make sure we arrest Mr Enderby's killer this afternoon.'

'Words, words, words.'

McLevy replied harshly, 'Mr Douglas, I know your strongest wish is to protect Mrs Hatterton. If you don't allow me to arrest the murderer you will put her life in danger.'

Jack left the room.

'You are an unscrupulous devil, McLevy,' said Dr Sandy. 'Would you really bring all that to court?'

'I had to convince myself that I would. How else should I convince Mr Douglas?'

'Why didn't you ask him more about the deer head? You obviously thought it important.'

'Because I intend to hear the story from Mrs Hatterton.'

Dr Sandy's voice swelled with outrage. 'McLevy, I can't let you badger Alice, and no, you will not be allowed to see her on your own!'

'I shall *speak* to her alone, if Miss McLaren will kindly sit at the other end of this room.'

Chapter Thirty-five

Alice was wearing plain black silk, pinned all over with dark crepe. McLevy could see a resemblance to her mother today. Some nervous stress had left her and was now replaced by something he hadn't noticed before: a sense of grievance or resentment which had brought out the hitherto invisible likeness to Mrs Enderby.

He chose his position carefully; distant enough to reassure Miss McLaren who was sitting vigilantly at the other end of the library, but making sure that Alice need not raise her voice.

She opened the conversation herself. 'You will not be surprised to learn that we mean to sell Kilcorrie after we reach London.'

This was his most hazardous interview in the whole Enderby case. Should she pretend surprise he would have failed again. Alice remembered more than she had told Jack Douglas; but not all. If he was wrong – if he loosed all those memories for nothing – it would lie on his conscience for ever. He was gambling on what he had learned about the three young people. If he held back he would be letting the killer go free.

'You are the only person who can solve the riddle of the two murders in this house, Mrs Hatterton. You may refuse to answer my questions, but every question has a purpose.'

Alice nodded seriously, and said she would try to do

what Mr McLevy wished.

'Do you remember what happened at Kilcorrie in October of 1860?'

He waited anxiously. Alice considered his question without any sign of emotion.

'Since my father's death those events have returned to me very clearly.'

'Are you prepared to tell me about them?'

Alice looked at him thoughtfully. 'Yes, provided you do not question me too closely, Mr McLevy. It is difficult enough to begin my marriage in such dreadful circumstances. I should not wish to conceal anything from my husband. He will certainly ask me about our conversation.'

'I promise to confine my enquiries as you wish. May I prompt you? One morning in mid-October you received a serious fright.'

Alice nodded gravely. 'That is correct.'

'Your mother tried to persuade you to tell her, but she was unsuccessful. Forgive me if I seem too familiar.'

'You appear to know a great deal already,' replied Alice. 'However, you are mistaken in one point. Mama followed him into the room and saw what happened.' She was searching for details. 'I am not sure how much.'

'Might I ask you to describe everything from the beginning?'

'I was wakened very early by a clattering on the stairs. My bedroom is near the gallery.'

He listened to the bell-clear voice with a sensation of skin crawling at the back of his neck. His dog must experience something similar when her hackles rose. Alice sat upright; her eyes had become as shallow as those of a porcelain doll.

'I rose in bed and felt a stabbing pain below my waist. Mama says I should not discuss such matters with gentlemen.' Her eyes swivelled towards McLevy; there was still no expression in them.

'I shall pass on to what happened next. The door of my room was thrown open and I saw an animal with the head of a deer and a man's body.'

'That was only your first impression.'

Alice smiled. 'Of course. It was my father carrying the doe's head into my room. He ran over to the bed, laughing and panting. The blood from its neck was dripping down his hands. He flung himself on the bed and pulled me towards him. Then he kissed me. He was very excited.'

'Yes.' McLevy's throat began to go dry. He had cramp in his right leg but dared not move it.

'Well, really, that is all,' said Alice with a slight shrug. 'I cannot remember how long my father stayed in the room. He kept on kissing me, and then kissing the doe's mouth, and kissing us both together. It was rather silly, wasn't it? When he went out I pushed the deer head underneath my bed.'

'You said your mother came into the room.'

'Oh, yes. Later I realised Mama had been there a long time, but I didn't notice her until my father put on his shooting jacket. I helped him button it up. When we turned round, Mama was standing in the doorway.'

McLevy heard the unsteadiness in his own voice as he asked,

'Did you describe this incident to Mr Douglas?'

'To Jack?' Alice gave the question earnest thought. 'I believe I did, but not in such detail. As I said, it was all very silly. Sometimes my father behaved like a child.'

She stood up and held out her hand. 'Goodbye, Mr McLevy. I do not care to leave Mama too much on her own, and my husband will be anxious about me.'

'I am sorry to have kept you so long.' McLevy could hardly get his tongue round the words.

'There is one more thing,' he said, as she went towards the library door. 'Miles Hatterton is not your husband, Miss Enderby.'

Chapter Thirty-six

McLevy waited for Sergeant Kincaid's helmet to rise into sight on the library stairs. The sergeant said,

'There's word come by the post-gig that Mrs Maxwell's found her brooch. It was in a bonnet box.'

'Poor Jimmy!' McLevy smiled. 'We'll let him free after he's served our turn.'

'Dinna be sorry for him, sir. The Dunfillan chaps say he beats his wife.'

McLevy had decided to take Jimmy to Kilcorrie only after hearing the details of what he had seen in the wood. The first plan had been to leave him at the inn with Sergeant Kincaid, in case he said something to spring the trap too soon.

Jimmy had not recognised the figures he saw among the trees, nor witnessed the actual murder. Everything else had been wiped from his mind by that one episode.

At first this was a disappointment to McLevy. Later, he had seen a way to turn it to his advantage. Now he said to Sergeant Kincaid, 'Make sure Jimmy holds his tongue till he has the cue to speak.'

'Oh, aye, sir, I've taught him well. Will we nab the other here as well?'

'I don't know yet, Johnnie, but it'll be some time this afternoon. He has no notion we're on to him.'

The officer murmured, 'I'd never credit it if you hadna telt me yourself.'

He had been repeating this remark in various ways ever since McLevy kept his promise to reveal the name of the young girl's killer.

The two men went down the library stairs. Dr McLaren was waiting for them in the hall.

'What on earth did you say to Alice? She looks like a ghost.'

McLevy shook his head and paused on the threshold of the dining-room. The other mourners had left, and the company was now reduced to seven. Mrs Enderby was seated on a couch by the nearest window and round her were grouped Alice, Mr Bisset, Miles, Jack, the procurator-fiscal, and Flora McLaren.

As well as the drapes of black crepe Mrs Enderby wore a widow's cap and streamers and had stripped off her finger rings. There were dull gleams of jet at her throat and bosom.

The group was posed as if in a photographer's studio, but their stillness was an illusion; the air was crackling with mistrust and anxiety. Alice was plucking at the folds of her skirt. She gave McLevy a quick glance and then dropped her eyes. He had extracted a promise that she would repeat only the bare message that he wished to speak to them together.

Jack hurried across to McLevy.

'You have meddled enough, McLevy! Why can't you leave us alone?'

The detective ignored him and walked towards Mrs Enderby's sofa, Dr Sandy hanging half a step in the rear.

'I did not expect to see you again, sir.' Her voice sounded even more tremulous.

Dr Sandy glared at McLevy as the dining-room doors closed with a heavy click and Sergeant Kincaid took up position in front of them.

'Mrs Enderby, I must tell you that your husband was killed by someone present in this room.'

The group responded slowly, apparently gripped by that dislocation of time which overtakes people during the ceremonies of death. Miles stirred on his feet, and John Maxwell blinked.

Mrs Enderby's eyes moistened as she whispered, 'Please do not ask me any more questions.'

The fiscal exclaimed, 'You could lose your pension for this, McLevy.'

'Mr Maxwell, I will stake my pension on this.'

Miles leaned back with his left forefinger touching his moustache. David Bisset reached out for a chair, and sat down in an oddly stealthy way. He began to rock to and fro, rubbing his knees.

'If Mr McLevy knows the murderer it is his duty to speak out.'

McLevy began, 'Ladies and gentlemen, Mr Maxwell shall hear full particulars later.' He took a look round the group, and was satisfied with their response. 'Both murders turn on the fact that the marriage between Miss Enderby and Captain Hatterton was irregular.'

Mrs Enderby clasped her daughter's hand. 'Sir, that is of little importance now.'

'I must show why these events happened, or no one will believe the charge... Mrs Vesey was murdered inside the deer larder soon after the sporting party set out. After some kitchen gossip about the status of the marriage, she told her fears to Mr Enderby. She was killed because of that conversation, but not by Mr Enderby.'

Lifting her head, Mrs Enderby whispered something too low for him to catch. He thought it was *Thank you.*

'The murderer was ruthless. He valued his pride more than the life of another human being.'

'You have put the ladies out of their suspense,' said Flora McLaren. 'I see you intend to accuse one of the gentlemen.'

The three women were seated in a row. McLevy gazed

at each in turn. 'I use the word *he* in the generic sense, Miss McLaren. Some female murderers are as cold-blooded as any man.'

Flora sat back.

'Captain Hatterton, I owe you an apology for wondering whether Mr Enderby's death was linked with your thirtieth birthday. We both believed your inheritance would lapse if you were married after that date.'

'Confound you, McLevy, there's no need to spell it out!'

Mrs Enderby stared in disbelief. 'Is that true, Miles?'

His reply was a confused mutter. 'Aunt Melton threatened and then didn't come up to scratch.'

'Mama,' pleaded Alice, 'we were wicked to treat you so, but let us not wrangle over that now!'

While they were recriminating, McLevy had made a signal to Sergeant Kincaid.

'Captain Hatterton's birth date, the first day of September, is registered in Somerset House. The question I posed does not arise.'

Uneasy smiles appeared on their faces. Apparently none of them had heard the doors open again. Jimmy Dewar was now standing beside Sergeant Kincaid.

'Captain Hatterton and Miss Enderby were to marry under the Brougham Act of 1856. This preserves the legality of marriage by declaration, but the union is valid only if one of the parties has resided in Scotland for twenty-one days.'

McLevy put a hand to his breast pocket.

'This report has been cut from a news journal dated the twelfth day of August.'

'Grouse on the wing,' quipped Dr Sandy.

'It winged my own thoughts, and I am hopeful it may wing the person who killed Mr Enderby.'

McLevy turned back to Alice. 'Two days before, the railway lines outside York buckled because of intense heat. The special Scotch Express ran off the line after the luncheon halt at York, a few minutes before three o'clock, only a hundred yards beyond the station.'

Jack shouted, 'Stop baiting her!'

Alice said, 'You have frightened me for nothing, Mr McLevy. We continued our journey from York some hours after the accident.'

'I assumed you would board the night express. I think you slept until it arrived in Edinburgh Station about half past eight the next morning.'

'Yes,' Alice said wonderingly. 'Why is that significant?'

'Even a parliamentary train cannot take nine hours to reach Edinburgh from Berwick-on-Tweed. The distance is ninety miles. You must have crossed the Royal Border Bridge well after midnight. You had not resided twenty-one days in Scotland – *twenty-one complete days* – until September 2nd.'

Alice's face cleared. 'Today is the 6th. We need only state again that we are married.'

Miles said, 'Now look here, McLevy -'

Mr Maxwell pulled the detective aside. 'Habit and repute,' he muttered. 'And – er – the rest.' His face took on a look of horror.

McLevy whispered, 'There has been no *rest*.'

'Then let us keep to the main question,' Mr Maxwell retorted icily. They turned back to the company.

'Mr Douglas, you realised the implication of the railway accident and wrote about it to Captain Hatterton. I suspect the two days he spent in Edinburgh were to check your facts. There was an elaborate ceremony on September 1st, but both of you knew it was invalid.'

Miles burst out, 'McLevy, you aren't fit for decent company. You deserve to be skinned!'

'The two of you agreed that the captain would keep bachelor quarters until the second declaration on Friday. You intended to execute it so informally that Miss Enderby would not realise what was happening.'

Jack's face turned a dull red. Alice was looking bewildered.

'After listening to some kitchen gossip Mrs Vesey also realised that the marriage was illegal. She rushed out to tell Mr Enderby immediately before the tinchel.'

Miles smoothed his moustache, and smiled. 'What a fuss over nothing.' He put his right hand on Alice's shoulder.

McLevy went on, 'Mr Enderby had of course known that the marriage was irregular, but not that it was invalid. He broke the news to Captain Hatterton. I assume you would echo his horror, sir, and then reassure him with some version of your pact with Mr Douglas. You went to the kitchen to track down Mrs Vesey, who had gone up to her room. After ringing for her from the library, you both went to the deer larder to look for your seal.'

Deliberately, he did not complete the story.

Miles laughed. 'Good enough for a fair, McLevy! Why should I kill poor old Abby?'

'To stop her chatter, here and at York. You were also afraid that your aunt's solicitor might find out the facts I've described, and that would rob you of your inheritance. As it happened, Mrs Melton had cancelled the proviso about your birthday, but by the time you knew that you had also murdered Mr Enderby.'

Miles laughed even more heartily.

'Do you deny these facts, sir?'

A fissure of doubt ran across the smiling, self-assured face. McLevy nodded to Sergeant Kincaid, who pushed forward Jimmy Dewar. McLevy felt in his pockets.

He let the gold seal drop on a small round table beside the sofa, and waited.

Miles walked forward and picked up the seal. 'By Jove, theft as well as slander.'

McLevy threw down a scatter of hairpins. Miles stood looking at them.

The next item was covered by McLevy's wrist and fingers. He called over his shoulder,

'Do you recognise him, Jimmy?' He hoped justice would forgive the lie.

'Aye, yon chap you're talking to. I watched him do it.'

'Do what, you fool?' demanded Miles.

McLevy turned his palm upwards and unwrapped his handkerchief from the open razor.

'What you did with this, Captain Hatterton.'

Miles stared down at the rusty blade and then snatched the razor from McLevy's hand. He ran to the French windows with his arms wrapped round his head. In a splintering of glass and wood he broke through it to the terrace.

The four men rushed to the shattered window. Jack Douglas wrapped a fold of curtain round his right hand and punched the remaining fangs of glass from the frame. He stepped outside, followed by the others. They dashed to the balustrade.

Miles Hatterton was already halfway across the parkland, running as fast as a deer.

Chapter Thirty-seven

It was John Maxwell who let out the staghounds.

Jack took a message to the policemen billeted at Inverconan: they were to cordon off the ford across the Crannich. Sergeant Kincaid told the fiscal he would set a guard on the bridge by Kilcorrie village.

'It looks like our other business will have to wait,' he said to McLevy on his way out.

The menservants spread over the parkland and walked in a line towards the river. While the fiscal was giving them orders Dr Sandy took a rifle and cartridges from the gun room.

'Hatterton may try the salmon pools. We must prevent him slipping into the hills.'

Alice said in a low voice, 'Miles cannot swim.'

McLevy was sure that no one else had heard her. Her eyes looked almost black; they were glistening as they travelled from one man to another.

The air was full of shouting and the banging of doors; men ran in and out of the building. Hours seemed to pass, but in reality the disconnected figures had formed themselves into a group while Miles was still visible at the edge of the park. The staghounds had almost overtaken him.

David Bisset stood up. 'My presence may be needed.'

In at the kill, thought McLevy with distaste, remembering the look on the clergyman's face while he was unravelling the murders. He stayed in the room until Mr Bisset had left. When there were only himself and the three women, he glanced at Flora McLaren.

She said, 'Miss Enderby would prefer her mother to be spared as much of this as possible. I shall go upstairs with them.'

McLevy was walking towards the door when Alice called after him, 'Wait, Mr McLevy!'

She continued to walk out of the room beside him. In the hall, to his great surprise, she offered her hand.

'If my mother were able she would join me in giving you our thanks for proving my father's innocence. You have lifted a terrible burden from us, Mr McLevy.'

He had never studied a face so hard. Could mere manners hide such a wound, let alone heal it? Surely not. Violence had either scourged out all emotion or had been strangely cathartic. There were no traces of the anger he had glimpsed a few moments before.

He went to the kitchen to collect Jeanie Brash. Only Jimmy Dewar and the cook remained in the room; the other servants had gone to watch what was happening in the park.

'You can go home now, Dewar. The brooch has been found.'

Jimmy said sullenly, 'It was you brought me, so you can just take me back.'

He had delivered his lines well. McLevy felt he owed him something. He took out his note book and wrote a short message.

'If you make haste you'll catch the station omnibus. Take this to Mistress Gregory. She'll give you the fare.'

'You're a Christian, Mr McLevy'.

The detective's mouth turned down. 'I'll be the devil himself if I hear more of you hanging around Janet McIver.'

Jimmy snatched up his cap and darted out of the room.

The Crannich was swollen from Saturday night's rain. McLevy could hear it roaring in the gorge. He was not more than a hundred yards from the Kilcorrie gates when a blue-uniformed figure came running along the road.

'They've found him!'

McLevy puffed along at the side of the young constable. At the steepest crook of the road the fiscal was sitting in Miles Hatterton's smart green gig. It was surrounded by a jabbering knot of men who were bunched against the earthen bank, although their heads kept turning towards the other side of the road. The hindquarters of the staghounds were making the leaves quiver as they whined and scrabbled above the abyss.

In the group were more policemen and Dr Sandy. One of the officers had his right arm out of its sleeve and roughly bandaged.

'He's gone down to the rock,' said Dr Sandy. 'The dogs are too frightened to follow.'

The fiscal said, 'They were only to lead us to him.'

Dr Sandy picked his rifle out of the gig. 'We've tried shouting to Hatterton, but he won't answer.'

'Are you sure he's there?'

'Mr Bisset went down to the river with a constable. They saw him quite distinctly.'

'Show me, please.' McLevy secured Jeanie Brash to a wheel of the vehicle.

Another policeman offered to guide him. They walked towards the village, and where the road began to flatten out the officer pointed across the road.

'Yon's the path down to the water, sir. It's slippy, but if you hang on to the roots you'll be all right.'

As they were about to step off the road, the minister appeared on the path below them, pushing his way through the leaves.

He said, 'I have tried to approach the rock, but it is

impossible along the edge of the water. It looks as if Hatterton is trapped there.' He began to walk back towards the pass.

McLevy lowered himself over the fallen trunks and found a well-worn track, perhaps used by children or poachers. It led along the bank to the open end of the gorge, where the river began to flow over a bed of sand and gravel. Grass and weeds swayed under the water; it had risen several inches above its usual level.

'Where is he?' he shouted against the noise.

'Look on to yon rowan tree, sir, and the crag it stands on.'

McLevy stared upstream; the Crannich surged giddily towards him, smooth tongues of treacle-dark water alternating with the thunderous eddies of foam.

The river had carved its gorge into monstrous profiles; only by comparing them with the height of the trees could the eye reduce them to their proper scale. McLevy scanned a dozen rowan trees weighed down with scarlet berries; his gaze halted at one that grew out of a huge cube of stone narrowing towards its base. From the side facing the river projected a narrow ledge; a man was crouching there.

'I see him now. Can they not drop on him from above?'

'Constable Niven went down on a rope, sir, but the captain slashed him with the razor.'

'Several of us must go down together.'

Another constable scrambled over the boulders from the road. 'Sir! Mr Maxwell says could you come back at once.'

McLevy returned to the road with the two policemen.

Dr Sandy was standing at the top of the path, grasping his rifle. He said in an argumentative tone, 'We can't leave him there till dark. Hatterton will jump across.'

'He'd kill himself if he tried!'

'No such luck, McLevy. There's a table of rock on the other side, six or ten feet lower. Why d'you suppose he took himself to Mackenzie's Leap? You try to talk some sense into Maxwell.'

When they reached the gig the fiscal was sitting in it smoking a cigar. He threw Dr Sandy a baleful look. 'Well?'

'What is the dispute, gentlemen?' McLevy asked.

Dr Sandy tapped the barrel of his rifle. 'I say we give Hatterton one hour to surrender, and if he won't, we bag him from the other side.'

'Good God, McLaren, we can't shoot him like a mad dog.'

'Better than endangering more of your own men.'

Mr Maxwell glared, and turned away. 'Talking of dogs, McLevy, your animal has been howling like a banshee.'

McLevy bent down to pat Jeanie, who was sitting docilely where he had left her, tied to one wheel of the gig. He looked round the group. 'She's quiet enough now. Those two great brutes must have frightened her.'

The fiscal returned to his quarrel with Dr Sandy.

'Your fire-eating so alarmed Mr Bisset that he's down there now, trying to persuade Hatterton to come up.'

The doctor growled, 'That's his own decision, sir.'

Mr Maxwell lifted the reins of the gig. 'I shall drive across the river. Will you come with me, McLevy?' He turned to one of the policemen. 'Shout down to Mr Bisset. Reassure him we're only going for a better view.'

'Very good, sir.'

The fiscal said coldly, 'Come with us if you like, McLaren, but you'll have to leave your gun behind.'

Chapter Thirty-eight

Every twelve feet the rope was knotted around the close-growing trunks. They were lichened and oozing with damp, some so rotten that the constable's weight had snapped them when he descended. Their broken-off fragments were caught in the knots like rungs of a ladder, and provided a treacherous foothold. Between them, David Bisset had to slide down the wet bank.

After a few yards his hands were scorched; the muddy rope kept slipping through them and the roar of the unseen water became more terrifying as he approached it. He wedged himself in the fork of a tree. Looking up through the foliage, it was impossible to judge how far had he descended. His legs were trembling from their resistance to the downwards pull.

After a few moments' rest he swung himself out from the tree and began to descend hand over hand. It was easier if he leant outwards. The metallic smell of wet rock rose up more strongly. There was something different about the feel of the rope; he braced himself against its tautness, but it no longer held between the knots. It was dangling free; he had nearly reached its end.

He jammed himself again, and peered down. Below was a flat-topped rock where a spindly rowan tree had rooted itself. Now the rope had run out; he would have to let go.

David Bisset made a grimace of self-disgust, shut his

eyes, and took his hands off the rope.

By grabbing at roots and clumps of leaf mould, he managed to brake his slithering descent to the edge. His foot went through a cushion of moss; there was a foot-wide gap between the bank and the inner face of the rock. The rock was far higher than it had looked from downstream, rising at least twenty feet above the river. He stepped across the gap and clutched at the trunk of the rowan tree.

He felt dizzy with relief. The small plateau was covered with earth and grass. At least it was wider than it had looked from above. He pulled his fingers off the bark, and forced himself to the lip of the rock, where he crouched on his knees.

His first glance at the tumbling swirl below produced a spasm of vertigo. He had to lean back, shutting his eyes. When he looked again he saw the top of Miles Hatterton's head.

The roar of the water was deafening; the serrations of rock almost broke through its glossy smoothness. No one could be dragged through those stone teeth and live.

'Captain Hatterton!'

He had to cup his hands and shout twice. The head turned and stared up at him. He lay flat on the grass and pushed himself a few inches forward.

'Captain Hatterton, you must give yourself up. They will shoot you if you remain on this rock. You must not die with such sins on your conscience. Think of your immortal soul.' He was thinking of his own.

There was no reply. The head did not move; the eyes showed flinty contempt.

'Providence is more merciful than earthly justice. Leave yourself time to repent. Let us go up together.'

Miles Hatterton now leant outwards, his fingers thrust into crevices on the face of the rock. The whole upper half of his body had become visible but he still did not speak.

David Bisset tried again. 'Our Lord said, Bear ye one another's burdens. Help me to as brave as yourself, Captain Hatterton. My transgressions are as vile as yours.'

There was still no response.

The minister's voice changed to urgent informality. 'Dr McLaren is driving to the rock on the other side of the river. He'll be there in a few moments. He's going to shoot you.'

The eyes blinked, and Miles began to pull himself to the top of the rock.

Joyfully, David Bisset held out his hand, but Miles bounded rather than scrambled over the edge. He was grasping the open razor as he flexed his cramped fingers.

'Stand back, parson!'

He took three paces to the inner side of the rock and in passing stroked the razor round David Bissset's neck. He stretched out his arms, took a springing hop, and launched himself across the river.

McLevy and Dr Sandy walked back to the captain's green gig.

'We must wait for Maxwell,' said the doctor. 'What a mess!' He kicked at the oat stubble.

When they reached the viewpoint on the far side of MacKenzie's Leap they had seen Miles Hatterton throw himself off the rock. He had missed by several feet.

McLevy lifted Jeanie Brash up to the gig and climbed beside her. 'Is there any chance he'll come out alive?'

'After a minute in there he'll be *disiecta membra* like Medea's little brother.'

The procurator-fiscal came tramping towards them flanked by two policemen. They listened to a brief order, and then headed across the shorn field.

John Maxwell climbed into the gig with a set face. After a moment's silence he said, 'He certainly had pluck.'

'Will you be able to pick up what's left of the body?'

'I've told the officers to search as far down as New Nisbet. It may stick in the mill-race there. I don't want it to frighten the washerwomen.'

The fiscal picked up the reins and urged the pony forward. He took them slowly across the fields, and at a quicker pace when they had crossed the bridge. He did not speak again until they were passing through the village.

'I hope that constable persuaded Mr Bisset to return to the road.'

The men were still waiting at the point where the minister had gone down among the trees. The two staghounds were no longer with them; one of the policemen said they had been taken back to Kilcorrie.

The fiscal announced that Captain Hatterton had tried to jump the river and had been swept downstream. There were murmurs of surprise.

'Where's Mr Bisset? Has he gone home too?'

Sergeant Kincaid said, 'He's still downby, sir. We heard voices, but we didna ken what was happening. We thought he was still arguing with the captain.'

'We didn't see him on the rock.' Mr Maxwell took a tight grip of a hazel branch and leaned cautiously over the green depths. 'Be silent, everyone!... I can hear someone groaning. It must be Bisset.'

'I'll go down, sir,' said McLevy suddenly.

'You? Let one of these young lads do it.'

'Send Sergeant Kincaid after me. If Mr Bisset is hurt he'll need to be lifted up.' He said to the sergeant, 'Bring two constables with you, but first give me ten minutes alone with him.'

Sergeant Kincaid nodded. McLevy turned himself round and clasped both hands round the rope. Jeanie Brash whined in panic. He grinned up at her.

'Show your spirit, lass. You're not feared of a wee scramble, are you?'

As he let himself down, inch by inch, Jeanie slid down

beside him. She soon learned it was easier to go backwards.

At the end of the rope McLevy braced himself between two alders, after testing their soundness. He peered down and saw the black-coated figure stretched out beneath the rowan tree.

He took the rest of the descent unhurriedly, and then stepped across the gap in the moss. He knelt down. Blood was seeping from a deep gash in the minister's neck, but McLevy did not think it was fatal. He hunkered down and brought out a handkerchief which he laid over the wound. The minister opened his eyes.

'You did a brave thing, Mr Bisset. I wish it were sufficient amends, but we both know it is not.'

David Bisset groaned and rose on his left elbow. He looked at Jeanie Brash, flattened on the grass behind McLevy. The smell of blood had driven her back and she was lurking behind her master with bared teeth.

'I suppose it was your dog, Mr McLevy.'

'That's only half of it. You write too fine a hand, Davie lad. Mr Grantly Carmichael turned you off without a recommendation, didn't he?'

There was a faint nod.

'You wandered into bad company when you left Elgin for Edinburgh.'

'That was not my intention.' The words were a painful whisper. He closed his eyes again.

McLevy looked down at the sprawled figure, regretting that there had to be a streak of cruelty in any triumph. He always felt a sense of disgust towards the end of a case. It was partly the slip-shod brutality of events, and partly that he enjoyed the chase too much.

'Whisky's the best blindfold, Davie, and you'd taken the taste for it in Elgin. When you heard that Mr Macdonald was dead you wrote to Constantinople. You believed you were as good as on the way to your folk and manse in

Glencrannich. Never boast about dinner till the rabbit's in the pot. Was it early May you had his refusal?'

Another weak nod.

'I thought so. Just before the General Assembly of the Kirk, and the drowning accident. You must have been in despair. Debt, crime – and then killing yon bairn.'

The tortured eyes opened and looked up at him. 'I did not mean to kill her. I was afraid you would catch me.'

'You put a deal of work into your forged testimonial, but that would be a bagatelle after the Sanders lassie.'

The assault on the child had sprung from panic; the request for Mr Grantly Carmichael to recommend 'this worthy young man' to the Earl of Dunfillan was a planned deception. The High Court would have to weigh the gravity of each act against its outcome. Not his responsibility, thank heaven.

McLevy stood up. Sergeant Kincaid and the two policemen were crashing through the branches above.

'Come, Davie, we must help you to the upper regions.'

David Bisset had not heard him. His eyes were shut again. McLevy bent down as he saw that the lips were trying to speak.

'Not just the dog. Who told you?'

Mr Liston, the minister at Luncarty, had provided some useful dates. He was clerk to the Perth Synod and held information on all the ministers in his area. As well as the forged testimonial the Kilcorrie estate boxes had contained a letter purporting to be from Mr Grantly Carmichael to the earl. McLevy had the paper in his pocket. That was all matter for the High Court.

'No one told me, Mr Bisset. You should have discarded all your clerical garments when you fell among thieves. My mind's eye sees it this very minute – the Royal Mile during the General Assembly, and the ministers walking up and down it in their black side-buttoned waistcoats.'

Chapter Thirty-nine

The Enderby house party, David Bisset, the procurator-fiscal and his policemen, and Jimmy Dewar, had all left Glencrannich. McLevy resolved to spend the rest of his holiday in learning to fish.

Donald had been released from Dunfillan gaol on the Wednesday after Mr Enderby's funeral. McLevy was present at a family celebration in the Dunfillan Arms. It took place at noon, so that the youngest McIvers could attend.

'There's aye something,' said Mrs Gregory philosophically, when McLevy remarked that Hector looked no more reconciled to his brother's marriage. 'It needs no second sight to tell that Hector will have left the glen by the end of the year.'

'What about the croft?'

Mr Maxwell had assured McLevy that removing the threat of eviction was the least possible recompense. He would see to it when the estate was settled.

'Rory and Jamie are growing lads. They and Janet will manage fine,' said Mrs Gregory.

There never was more than a half mending, McLevy told himself. Like his own half fancies, when Janet McIver smiled at him from the end of the table and he wished himself thirty years younger.

At seven o'clock on the following Saturday evening he

was settling down for a glass of ale in the taproom. He had eaten his first catch. Only a small trout, but he had been invited to try his luck with the Balinmore salmon beat. Jeanie was dozing at his feet. Dr Sandy appeared at the taproom door.

'I have the parlour to myself, McLevy. Come and join me at table.'

'I'll join you with pleasure, but I've eaten my supper.'

They talked about David Bisset. McLevy admitted that the case had been eased by the minister's own guilt and confession. The charge would be homicide, rather than murder.

'You're deuced lucky, McLevy, aren't you? You were bluffing about the other as well.'

'What do you mean?' He hoped to avoid the final explanation.

'All that mumbo-jumbo about what Jack Douglas told Hatterton. Quite unnecessary.'

'As you say.'

'Very weak! No wonder you didn't mention the incident at the tinchel to John Maxwell. I shall turn your own reasoning against you. Why should Enderby even think of telling Mr Clark that the marriage would not be valid until the next day? Of course he wouldn't! Nor would Mrs Vesey.'

'You are quite right, Dr McLaren.'

Dr Sandy hit the table. 'There you are! It was guesswork.'

McLevy was piqued, but held his tongue.

The doctor asked suspiciously, 'You're sure it was Miles who killed them?'

'As surely as he fell into the Crannich.'

'Hmph!'

McLevy sighed. 'Perhaps I shall tell you for the sake of your sister's friendship with Mrs Enderby. Do you think Alice Enderby will marry young Douglas?'

'Very probably, after the year of mourning. What's that

to do with my question? You're dodging again, McLevy!'

'We both made wrong assumptions. I supposed Alice Enderby was with child, and you – didn't you believe she helped mutilate her father's body?'

Dr Sandy growled, 'The events threw my judgement off balance.'

'I am not expressing a moral opinion, Balinmore.'

Dr Sandy frowned and pursed his lips.

'Why did we think so meanly of Miss Enderby, though we neither loved nor hated her? At the tinchel Miles Hatterton made a half-hearted attempt to kill Mr Enderby, because he wanted to prevent his meeting Mr Clark. A few hours later he had murdered him and performed a barbaric mutilation. Why?'

'There was more risk at the tinchel.'

'He was an expert shot. In all that confusion, he could have contrived it. No, he did not have the will to murder Mr Enderby until his quarrel with Jack Douglas.'

'What do you mean?'

'Young Douglas told me a story about a ferret. The gist was that Miles killed it because someone else had used it.'

'Jack was trying to blacken Hatterton.'

'Of course, but the details would be correct. I hoped our evidence was sufficient to convict Hatterton of both murders. If not, my hand would have been forced. The ferret story convinced me he would do away with her in Italy. That was looking back, of course, after I heard about the deer head and put both stories together.'

'You're topsails over the horizon now, McLevy. I do not follow.'

'Alice Enderby told young Douglas only as much as she could bear to remember about the deer head.'

'That's fanciful, McLevy.'

'Then you do not listen very closely to your patients. I realised the story might convey a great deal more to me than to Jack Douglas.'

Dr Sandy rubbed his hands. 'I persuaded Flora to be indiscreet. Rose Enderby told her about the deer head years ago. A pretty grisly thing for a young girl to find underneath her bed.'

'You have the wrong story, Dr McLaren. Mrs Enderby did not tell your sister the truth.'

Word for word, McLevy repeated his conversation with Alice.

'If Jack Douglas had understood what he was being told he certainly would not have repeated it to Miles Hatterton, and Mr Enderby might have been alive today. That's why he shares responsibility for his death.'

Dr Sandy muttered, 'I still do not follow.'

'After hearing the story of the deer, Miles Hatterton formed a certain idea, if one may use so intellectual a phrase about his response. He killed Mr Enderby and mutilated the corpse because he thought that Alice had been violated by her father.'

Dr Sandy said, 'Now I see what you meant about our assumptions! Was Hatterton insane? I suppose he must have been. His actions prove it. No wonder he jumped to the wrong conclusion.'

McLevy carefully filled his pipe.

'Dr McLaren, we shall never know whether it was the wrong conclusion.'